CW01654233

GOOD NIGHT, MR MOON

Barbara Hanrahan was born and grew up in Adelaide, and was living there at the time of her death in 1991. A leading printmaker as well as novelist, she went to London in the early 1960s to study at the Central School of Art, and has taught in art schools both in England and Australia. She has had many one-woman exhibitions and her work appears in the Australian National Gallery and most state galleries. Her first book, *The Scent of Eucalyptus*, was published in 1973, and *Iris in Her Garden* by Officina Brindabella in 1991 (and UQP in 1992). Barbara Hanrahan is now the author of two collections of stories and twelve novels, including *Where the Queens All Strayed* (UQP, 1978), *The Peach Groves* (UQP, 1979), *The Frangipani Gardens* (UQP, 1980), *Dove* (UQP, 1982), and *Flawless Jade* (UQP, 1989).

Other books by Barbara Hanrahan

The Scent of Eucalyptus
Sea-green
The Albatross Muff
Where the Queens All Strayed
The Peach Groves
The Frangipani Gardens
Dove
Kewpie Doll
Annie Magdalene
Dream People
A Chelsea Girl
Flawless Jade
Iris in Her Garden

BARBARA HANRAHAN

GOOD NIGHT, MR MOON

University of Queensland Press

First published 1992 by University of Queensland Press
Box 42, St Lucia, Queensland 4067 Australia

Typeset by University of Queensland Press
Printed in Australia by The Book Printer, Victoria

Promotion of this title has been assisted by the South Australian Government through the Department for the Arts and Cultural Heritage.

Cataloguing in Publication Data
National Library of Australia
Hanrahan, Barbara, 1939-91.
Good night, Mr Moon.

I. Title.

A823.3

ISBN 0 7022 2339 5

Granpa Rodda came from Redruth in Cornwall. He sailed to South Australia on the *Buffalo*, and was one of the boys who pushed Governor Hindmarsh's dog through a porthole into the sea; but, being a vice-regal dog, the ship was turned about and a boat lowered to rescue it. Granpa's photo's in the Town Hall at Beauville, and he built those houses like they have in England with the white stone round the windows. He built them in a row in the flashest part of Beauville, and then they gave him the privilege of naming the new street they'd outlaid, and he called it Redruth Street because of where he came from.

Granma Rodda came from up in the Hills, where they grow all the fruit and stuff. She was only a little lady, a very dainty person.

Mum's parents came from the Bavarian Mountains – their families were up there in the beginning of time, almost; they were up there when Adam and Eve were born, just about. Granma and Granpa Hoff were a very high class sort of German people, not the peasants that lived down in the fields.

Mum's mother had ten children. Mum said she'd had enough of kids before she even got married, so she only had me.

I was born that day in 1901 when the Duke and Duchess of York came. My father-to-be (he wasn't quite my father) was driving them in their carriage, and they were on calendars and teatowels and cups and plates. And Mum wanted to see the Duchess, only I like to think of her as the Queen, but I was nearly on the way. The lady next door thought it a bit dangerous, because the big road from Glenelg was only little stones and all rough, and it was a good few miles to Adelaide, and Mum might get a fright. But she wanted to see Dad-to-be driving the Queen – only she wasn't the Queen then, she was the Duchess who'd been Princess May of Teck. She wasn't known as Mary at all then.

The lady next door's children had a pony and one of those low carts with the big wheels kids had in days gone. She said Mum could have it if she could get one of the bigger boys out of the family to go with her, and if she started off early and took her time and didn't hurry perhaps she could make it.

Adelaide was full of people from everywhere, though lots of them were pickpockets and con-trick men come from interstate in disguise. Aborigines had been camped in the parklands for months ahead waiting to see the White King. The streets were full of flags, and Granpa Rodda was up with the other old colonists on their special stand. The Duke was a homing pigeon enthusiast, so two thousand pigeons waited to wing off in welcome from Victoria Square. And Mum had almost got to the Town Hall when the band started to play and she got excited: the Queen was coming, and so was I. Mum said she'd have to go home, and they had to turn round and go for their life. When they got back to Glenelg, Mum couldn't even get up out of the cart; they had to carry her and put her on the double bed, and I was born. If I'd come a bit earlier I would've seen the Queen in her hour-glass corset and high hair with its stiff, set, Princess May brow curl.

I was a fairly big baby. They called me Alexandra May. Princess May of Teck. Queen Alexandra was the Duke's mother who'd been Denmark's sweetest flower with sausage curls on her shoulders; and she grew a forest of roses and violets, and had a special affection for the bluebells down at Kew, and could play the piano and the harp and the dulcimer, and was a colour magician in needlework, and had a private cemetery for her favourite chow-chow dog friends. I'm proud of my name, Alexandra May . . . and I may, and then again, I may not.

My hair was naturally curly from when I was born, so Mum never did it up in rags: I had golden colour hair, all curls, as good as Queen Alexandra's; and Mum used to put one of my curls round her finger and pretend she had a new gold ring. I'd get down on my knees and Mum would wash my hair in the china bowl with Velvet soap, and then I'd shake my head and whizz and skip about till it was dry. And Mum had a puffing machine I could sometimes dry my hair with, and then I'd get a mountain of hair.

Mum had long golden-brown hair that hung on the ground if she sat on a stool. She had marvellous hair and she went to the big bloke in Rundle Street, a big high hair-man, and when her hair hung down wavy it just looked like a corrugated iron tank, and her mother had hair like it, too. When I was a kid I'd brush Mum's hair till my arms were nearly falling off. Mum'd sit on a stool and I'd brush her hair right down, because she couldn't reach to get to the bottom. And I'd brush it when she washed it and make it all nice and fluffy-up for her. Mum loved to have her hair brushed, and then she'd pin it up and make puffs and waterfalls; and she'd have a halo of little curls round her face, or plaits coiled into wheels round her ears, or one thick plait round her head with a velvet rose at the side.

Dad had a reddish colour moustache but he had black curly hair, shining like silver. (They had very good hair in those days – perhaps they ate things with olive oil in them.) But Dad didn't care for a lot of hair long, he wasn't one of those sissies. He had to be just beyond reproach with the people he worked for.

Dad had started off building houses with Granpa and their names were both Tom: Old Tom would build a house and Young Tom would build next door to him, till they'd run out of blocks of land. Then Dad had saved up enough to have thoroughbred racehorse-shaped horses and was driving the highest people in South Australia about in carriages. And when he drove the Duke and Duchess, their carriage was full of white York roses; and they invited Dad to their castle in England for afternoon tea; and the Duke had the toothache in the exact same molar that had been filled when he was in Adelaide twenty years before.

We lived at Glenelg, by the sea, where Granpa Rodda came in on the *Buffalo*; though in Granpa's young days the sea was right in – up past where the Post Office is now. And sand-hills were there years ago when they first came from England, and of course they had to carry the ladies in when they came off the boats, because they couldn't get over the water in their long skirts.

When I was a kid we used to go swimming, and some men went in the sea with no clothes on, and you'd see their blooming handle sticking out the front. But most people didn't take any notice if a man was showing a bit, because that was part of their life. If you were inclined to be rude you weren't allowed on the beach – you had to be a decent character to go naked where there was a mixed population. Though Mum was pretty fussy, oh cripes, yes – if Mum stood in the bath and wanted us to give her a rub-down or a massage, she'd put a towel round her hips and tie it up tight. She wasn't so fussy about her chest, but you couldn't help everything sometimes. But she never showed herself like that, and I bet she never stood up naked in front of my father in her life. And I never made any remarks about those things – about people showing their this, that, and the others, whatever. Because some kids pick on it, and right in the middle of some toffy stuff where you've got very nice people visiting, somebody just gets up and perhaps their skirt's caught and the kids'll see and say, "Oh, be careful – I can see your big bum." Who taught them it was a bum I don't know, but a lot of the boys used to say "Kiss your arse". Men call it that word more in preference any time, and it's just a sort of a word that's in the language. And then the kids say "Your tits are hanging out". You'd get a smack over your mug if you said that long ago.

Mum was very special, and you wouldn't have got anyone more religious than Granma Hoff – she might have belonged in the Bible. And Dad drove the Queen. And Granpa Rodda knew secret words, and had a pinny with gold fringes, and was a high-up member of the Freemasons' Lodge: he was a Handshaker; and he was just about the Mayor of Beauville five times, and built half the district from First to Fifteenth Street, and named Redruth Street where he lived on the corner in a house with a turret (and all the metalwork inside was something wonderful – everything was decorated with silver and brass, and the floorboards were all shiny, the furniture was all polished, and veined marble was let into all different places).

Granpa had been a boy in Cornwall who was always out rabbiting, and he'd had a greyhound and put the rabbits in his poacher's belt. But I only knew him when he was old with a white beard and a gold-topped cane and a flower buttonhole and a top-hat – though he still had his curly Cornish voice. Wherever he went he was accompanied by two liver-and-white cocker spaniels: Granpa's big legs could go, so I'd have to run to keep up with him and Lassie and Dash.

With my blue eyes and gold hair I was more like a doll than a child. I had a spotty muslin pinafore and a nice white starched collar and a little fur coat. I had a chain bangle and a seed-pearl necklace for going to church. I had a teddy-bear three feet high from France with real fur skin. I had a creamy pony that was like a big rocking-horse almost, but it wouldn't hurt you or anything. I rode it round our garden and down the beach, and I'd latch it on a post when I went inside. I fed it on lettuce leaves and apples, and Mum used to make some porridge sort of stuff.

We had a rabbit like a Persian cat – not an ordinary rabbit, but one with long wool as if it was an ancient animal. We had it for years, but some of those get nasty and bite.

Mum couldn't bear to get her garden dug up by dogs, and, though she liked cats, she didn't want me fiddling with a cat or putting it round my neck. You had to be more respectable with them. Mum wasn't keen on having a cat because she had valuable ornaments from overseas, and a cat might knock one over and break it.

Mum had a housekeeper-lady sometimes to do the floors, and we had polished floors and good carpets.

We had everything nice and clean, and everything right, because all our lot came from good families. And I always think – like the flowers, you come up from where things are decent.

Because Granma Hoff came from the Bavarian Mountains, she had a hobby of making plaster reindeer heads with the antlers like they had in the snow. She always wore a baby's bonnet sort of cap and she had little curls hanging down, and she'd shake her head when she was talking, and those curls wobbling and the cap used to make me laugh. She was a wonderful cook and she liked her wood-stove, and on the end it had a big thing to boil the water. Granpa Hoff made the fancy ironwork for the railways, and he'd come home from work of a night and take off his clothes down to his waist, and Granma would have the big tank hot and a bowl of water ready, and she'd wash his back out in the kitchen.

Though Granma and Granpa Hoff had all those children, they'd only lived with them in one of Granpa Rodda's small working people's houses in the ordinary part of Beauville. But they'd fitted everyone in correctly, and the kids had been brought up nicely, and hadn't been allowed to go out without permission or have anyone in or anything. It'd been pretty stiff living, and Granpa's leather strap had hung on the back of his chair, and the kids weren't allowed to talk at the table or poke or fiddle or help themselves – they'd had to ask permission; and if they'd had enough and couldn't have any more, they were told they'd had sufficient and to behave themselves.

And they went to Sunday School and sang in the choir and the boys grew up to be good tradesmen, and Hilda Hoff married Young Tom Rodda, and the other girls married very nice husbands, too, and they were all very polite people, very sedate, but if you asked them anything rude you'd get a smack in the nose.

Uncle William was a bricklayer. Uncle Henry was a carpenter. Uncle Maurice and Uncle Edward and Uncle Albert were highly qualified plumbers, and clever people for doing lavatories.

The girls were experts in roasting and boiling and grilling, and could use four knitting-needles at once. Aunty Eva was religious and had a mulberry nose and went to live in Western Australia. Aunty Minna was dreamy looking and got a funny thing in her blood. Aunty Rose played the piano. Aunty Albertina was artistic.

Aunty Albertina was famous for her painting "A Yard of Cats", and I counted them that many times: there were ten lying straight and two rolled together, and every cat was its own particular colour. She was Spanish-Frenchy looking, and married to one of the foremost chemists in town. If anybody was ill he could treat them without trouble or mischief of any kind, and he could straighten up babies that were born queer to get them right; but he kept snakes and lizards in cages, and Aunty Albertina was always scared they'd get out.

Aunty Rose had a black shawl embroidered with tiger-lilies, and its fringes tangled when she tossed it over the piano. I was allowed to play her piano, and I'd have to put a big Bible on top of the chair to get high enough. I couldn't put my feet on the pedals, but I could play a piece and sing a song exactly different at the same time.

Granma Hoff gave me a doll like the Sleeping Beauty for passing my first music exam. And her eyelids with spider's-leg eyelashes came open to show her glass eyes; and every piece of her body had proper human joints: fingers, wrists, ankles, knees, neck . . . You could stand her up or sit her down, and she said "Mama-Mama". With her real china face and golden sausage curls and little bosoms she was a perfect model of a thing that was alive. She came from England, and she had a blue pure silk hat and a blue pure silk dress and a blue velvet coat with braid round the edge. No ordinary child would have had a doll like that, and she must have been darn dear. I was surprised that Granma bought her, because those old German ladies – they're not spendthrifts.

Granpa Hoff was a very good gardener and planted lilies that came from far away up in the Islands. He reckoned a rooster crowing three times and a dropped dish-cloth were sure signs of visitors arriving. He had a carved wooden pipe and smoked strange kinds of tobacco, but one day he got up a ladder and fell down backwards and swallowed his false teeth, and then he died.

There was a rainbow in the sky just now, and rainbows are only shadows made by the sun and stars shining on the fluid up top — they've got no body in them. The moon was in the sky, too, but it was just a white clear thing, like it didn't even have its colouring. It wasn't exactly tiny, but it was up there; and the sun was up there as well. And the sun didn't have any colouring either. It was the most unusual mixture I've seen for a long time.

After Granma and Granpa Rodda died, Dad sold the horses and the carriages and the house at Glenelg, and we came up to the city to live. Our new house was right in Hopedene Street, near the Silver Dragon Hotel. It was a pretty house with a verandah and a carved front door, and Mum had dahlias and roses in the garden, but people pinched the flowers and once somebody pulled up a whole rose bush by the roots and took it (Dad thought someone might pinch Mum's china frog off the verandah, so he stuck it down with cement).

There was a fair strip of flower garden out the front, but not round the back: we had a lot of back yard, but that was where Dad kept his motor cars. You went up a little short street and along the back lane, and opened the two iron gates to get into the huge garage, and sometimes Dad had his whole six valuable cars parked there, and he had a pit with a lid where he could go down under and do work on his cars; and the cars got washed in our yard, so that was why Mum only had a back garden of pot plants (once Dad gave me a tyre that was no good any more, and I planted pansies inside it).

Dad had one of the first motor-car hire businesses in Adelaide. He had tons of cars: he had one of those cars — not the Rolls-Royce, but just below it. He had about the first Austin car in Australia; he had a steam car, most intricate . . . the best cars were the silver-grey and the golden-brown and the royal blue shades, and Dad had them all. But the royal blue car from Melbourne was hard to keep clean. Dust showed on it and the cats from the pub sat on the hood, and when you caught them they'd slide down the bonnet with their claws. Dad used to get cross – his cars were his children, almost.

The silver-grey car had white ribbons on the front for any very special big wedding; and Mum would put a white fringed summertime rug on the back seat for the bride to sit on, and a bunch of flowers that weren't too smelly and didn't drop their petals up by the back window, and a white mat on the floor for the bride to put her feet on. The car had been polished till you could just about see your face in any part of it, inside and out; Dad wore his navy blue suit and his cap with a peak, and I'd cleaned his best boots.

Dad was pretty well up with people that thought they were better than other people, and he got in a lot of places other people couldn't even open the door to and look in. He drove every sort of famous person of Adelaide about: Bishops and Judges and Generals; even the Governor and the Premier and the Lord Mayor. The Public Trustee's head lawyer always went with Dad, and they'd drive to estates in the country to make wills. South Australia's top explorer man absolutely trusted Dad, and they drove to faraway deserts and through dangerous forests. Sometimes Dad had to put chains on the wheels where the ground was all mud, and once they went into a cave and found a place where the naked Aborigines had been sitting, and there was a pattern of their bottoms from hundreds of years ago.

A lot of the famous people gave Dad presents. That man who had the superior winery up in the Hills would give him a bottle of very high champagne in a wickerwork basket

(Dad never drank any, but Mum didn't mind a sip with her roast dinner from a tiny glass you could only fit an egg in). That very old royal man – Sir Somebody – in the mansion with the tower at Mount Lofty would send Dad home with special smelly flowers from his garden for Mum. But Dad couldn't be shut in anywhere with a lot of flowers, particularly smelly scented – they made his head ache, so he'd always put them in the boot.

Dad was inclined to have headaches. He had greeny-brown eyes and if he went on a motor journey looking into the sun, or for a long time on a rough road, he'd get that sort of a head. Often when he got home he'd put the car in the garage, and run inside, and he'd be so bad he'd get undressed and hop into bed and he wouldn't want his tea.

I'd help Dad do the cars, and we'd polish the leather seats, and I'd tidy and dust, and sweep the carpets, and go round the tyres with a fine knife to get the little bits of pebble out so they wouldn't cut in. I had to do things properly or whatoh! – Dad was no fool.

The cars had a stand by the bank in Currie Street, and there was a telephone on a post so that if people wanted one they could ring there from their homes. Though half the time you couldn't get a car, because there'd be six others trying to ring through as well.

Dad couldn't do all the driving for the brides and the big blokes and the ordinary people himself, so he had several drivers, very responsible, to help. There were two chaps for the daytime driving who went to their own homes after work, and two night drivers who lived with us.

Sometimes, long past midnight, somebody might want a car in a hurry so there'd be a quick urgent call to us at home, and one of the drivers would have to go off. Dad usually answered the telephone, but now and then he and Mum would be out. The telephone was on a wall in the passage and if I heard it ringing, I'd jump out of bed and turn on the gas lamp and climb up on a chair so I was tall enough to answer it. I could take a message, or book a car, or tell Uncle Egbert and Uncle Alex in the sleepout that somebody wanted a car to come.

Uncle Egbert was one of Mum's cousins, and he was a nicely dressed young man the ladies liked to be driven by, because he was very good to arrange himself to drive carefully, and you could trust him – he never looked saucy and he wasn't a rude sort who went after the girls.

Uncle Alex was Dad's brother, and his name being Alexander and mine Alexandra we got on excellently well together. There's always a cheeky one in the family and Uncle Alex was an old daisy, and you could see he was cheeky from his little whiskers and his old-fashioned face. He was a great big strong man who loved children, and he'd play cricket with me and tell me a yarn, and I'd know darn well it wasn't true but he'd keep kidding me along with some funny thing.

From the time he was a little bloke he'd been a bit of a nuisance who was always climbing trees and falling out of them, and one day he took a horse of Granpa's and bolted off up to billyoh on it for two or three days.

Uncle Alex had gone on the track as a swagman with his blue cattle-dog pup in a billy-can. He still had his swag rolled up in the sleepout, and he said you could call it your drum or your knot or your bluey or your Matilda. And he still had his tin plate and pannikin and tuckerbag.

Uncle Alex said he'd padded the hoof thousands of miles, and had shared his campfire with Ned Kelly's brother. After he was robbed of his gold watch by a tea-and-sugar bushranger, he'd picked up a few bob singing "Ave Maria" outside Catholic churches and "Abide with Me" outside Church of England churches.

Uncle Alex could make plaited leather stockwhips and he reckoned he could knock a fly off a horse's earhole with his whip, without hurting the horse.

Mum hated emerald green and anybody who drank too much, but she liked her sip of high champagne and if she didn't feel right, or was getting a cold, she'd have a little bit of Tanunda brandy with something in it.

Dad wasn't hilarious, but a quiet man who drank pale ale with lemonade and smoked French scenty cigars and read good books and played the flute. He sang hymns on Sundays, but he never went to church. If you asked him to help you do something, he'd say his pet saying: "Which end's the middle?" He never interfered with what Mum told me to do – that was it: Mum was the boss.

Mum was a person with a strong personality, and you couldn't argue the point with her. She was serious on account of being German, and German people were strong-willed and sort of inside themselves; they were clever people, and clean, and their children had to behave. Mum was as good to me as she could be, but if I did something wrong I'd get smacked ears. If Mum put a dish of fruit on the table I couldn't go grabbing, and you weren't allowed to lick your fingers or wipe them on your serviette; and I wasn't allowed to say I wanted to go to the lavatory at the table, or push my chair back and knock someone over. When I got in a row I'd hide under Mum and Dad's double bed, right back by the wall.

Mum was a good cook who could cook umpteen-ten things. She'd do grilling or boiling or roast a nice chook, or steam it with parsley as Dad didn't like a lot of fatty stuff. She did coffee and rhubarb pie and Christmas puddings tied up in a cloth. And toffee date creams, fig and preserved ginger jam, those rolled-up pastry things with apricots.

Mum was an expert ballroom dancer, and an operatic coloratura soprano singer who'd won prizes. That sort of singing was a very difficult kind: you had to get up very high and know how to tip your voice up in the top of your palate to get the sound to go like an echo. Mum could sing those sharp songs where they went right up the top of the last note. She liked to sing "Killarney" and the other old Irish long-ago songs with a lot of trilly bits in them.

Mum wore lilies-of-the-valley pinned into her furs, and gold shoes and silk etceteras and satin evening dresses with spangles, that were small at the waist and came out in the skirt like a tent almost. Sometimes I'd help her put her corsets on, and she had summer ventilating corsets of netting she got from the Chinese man who went round selling from his two big boxes. Mum's corsets pushed her all up till she came out in front like a statue, and pulled her all in to make her little tiny waist.

Mum's Chinaman was called Yat-wing and he was a good-looking Chinaman, very gentlemanly, in a white shirt and a tie. He carried his boxes on a pole across his shoulders, and they were full of corsets and ribbons and lacy things and coffee essence and feather dusters and bath soap. Every so often he'd go home to see his wife in China, and he'd bring Mum back pinafores and petticoats and pants threaded with ribbon for me. Once he brought Mum some green eggs, but she didn't dare eat them.

The other night the moon looked like a big slice of watermelon. And last night the moon was like a sunset; it was absolutely red, as if it was on fire. And it was a whopper: a big round thing, like a balloon made of blood. And the sky was all moving, like a new day coming. But it was the night-time, because I'd got out of bed to look.

The gas lamp in front of our house in Hopedene Street was one of the best in the city. I was good friends with Mr Quigley, the lamplighter, who rode about on his bike with a long pole to light the lamps, and came to your house if your gas went wrong.

Our back lane ran off the little short street where the Quigleys lived, and Mrs Quigley was a beautiful ironer, and helped Mum with the washing and cooking for Uncle Egbert and Uncle Alex. She was a high religious person, and a nice-looking one, not exactly Salvation Armified, but going round the ancient ways of religion (Mum had something against the Salvation Army – she thought they were a lot of old cadgers who weren't as good as they morally were supposed to be). Mrs Quigley sang hymns and said prayers and read from the Bible in Victoria Square on Sundays.

Quigleys had a pet emu that poked its head over the fence, and a boy, Bertie, and two girls. They were properly behaved kids who weren't allowed to go two at a time to the lavatory or anything.

But the woman who lived next door to us was a cheeky bitch who'd go in the bath with her girlfriend. And her husband came home one day and caught them – they were both in the water with no clothes on, slopping round and splashing each other and having fun – and there was the hell of a row, and they both got a terrible cold in their tubes inside and were very sick girlfriends for a long time.

Hopedene Street could be a tricky place to live, because

the brewery where they made beer and the brown stout with the fluffy on the top wasn't far away, and there were often drunk men in the back lane, hiding around. And young men came delivering beer to the Silver Dragon and some of them were saucy buggers, a bit rude, and if they wanted to have a pee in a hurry, they'd just stand in the gutter doing it, and they wouldn't take any notice if you were looking. No children were supposed to go near the brewery, but lots of kids used to sneak in and then there'd be boys and girls having a look at each other or fiddling. The parklands was a bad place, too: Mum said there were a lot of dirty old men there, and if you went near them they'd have you.

Some Saturday afternoons Mrs Quigley would take me and Bertie and Gladys and Effie up to the Empire, that was the Bug House in Grote Street, and the kids there used to be awful – fighting in their seats and swearing out loud up the back of the high-up balcony, and you were meant to be decent when you watched the pictures, or they'd put you out. And Quig took us to see the Theatre Royal Christmas pantomimes – the ones with the girl in the Bush, and the Granma one, and the one with funny animals. Sometimes there was a tent by the market where a man had a Tivoli show, and there were fairy lights and Chinese lanterns, and we saw an Indian snake-charmer and a hypnotist and a lady with a crown of Parma violets and a lady with a whole white hen on her hat.

Once Quig took us to the Royal Waxworks and Palace of Wonders in the Rundle Street Arcade. We saw the heroes and bushrangers and criminals, and two girls from England who were absolutely joined together back-to-back. They stood back-to-back in front of a piano, and one played with her hands on the piano and the other played the violin, and yet they were joined together and when they walked they had four legs. And they were pretty girls with long yellow curls, both dressed nicely in white dresses with a frilly collar, and you had to pay to go in to see them. They were real people, but they were born joined together like that, and they grew up and they were still like it.

The night the comet came we were all out to watch, though some people kept their head under the pillow. I saw the comet with its two billion miles of tail flaming behind it — and it was just like a big finger writing with fire in the sky. Smart people were wearing comet dresses and having comet suppers and comet parties, and lots of people thought it was going to be the end of the world. It stayed up over Hopedene Street, growing fainter for nights, and because it wasn't the end of the world some religious people were disappointed. But so many things happened on account of the comet: Granma Hoff died, and Uncle Alex broke his leg, and Aunty Rose's tomatoes went off, and Aunty Albertina's grapes were no good, and Mum's new dress didn't fit.

Granma Rodda's sisters still lived up in the Hills, round Inglewood way, and sometimes I went to stay with Aunty Issie. She was a tiny old lady with a bump in her nose who wore sunbonnets and hadn't got married. She lived in a little square house that got the gully breezes, and I had a ha'penny every Saturday for washing the kitchen chairs out on the verandah.

I slept in a four-poster bed with all the frills on it and ate off a plate patterned with raised up forget-me-nots. Aunty Issie had pigs and fowls and a double-decker kind of a barn, and you could smell the apples as soon as you walked in. Her tiger apples were brown with a yellow stripe, and she had an egg-plum tree and there was the Orchard, the Vineyard, the Creek, and the Dell where it was damp with bluebells growing.

Old Ned, the horse, was thirty-two years old, though he still took us over to Aunty Dorrie's in the trap. But Aunty Dorrie told me off for eating too many cherries, and Cousin Dot was a queer person who'd gone like she didn't know anything, her mind was shut. She'd been that way for years, since the night her brothers put a candle in a skull with horns and hung it from the walnut tree. And they lit the candle and called Cousin Dot and she thought it was a ghostly thing floating, looking at her through the leaves, and she screamed and lost her mind and it never came back to her again.

There've been some big birds round lately, and they make a funny noise. I think they're coming from distant places because there's been such hot weather on account of the things in the sky coming down more, and we're gradually getting some of their heat, and all the grass and stuff the birds live on has been destroyed, and they're coming in and eating the vegetables and everything else we've got for ourselves. And this afternoon a huge aeroplane came over and it was that low I thought it was coming on the roof of the house. It made a terrible roar, and I could see all the screws and bolts where the wheels were hanging down. I've never seen one come so low. But they've got to now, because the air up in the sky is changing to heat so much, it's making the petrol stuff in the planes dissolve and they haven't got enough power left so they're falling and dropping near the roofs of people's houses.

I'd been brought up like a little lady, seeing one end of me was from the Bavarian Mountains and the other from

Redruth, Cornwall. I went to the Gilles Street School in a nice white pinny with lace round the yoke, and I had to shine my shoes and do everything properly. But some of the other kids at that school were pretty tough tigers from down the back streets of Adelaide; and they were rude and vulgar, they used to say a lot of nasty swearing words, they weren't very clean, they were common. One of those kids boasted how he was called Angas Elliot after two flash Adelaide judges (but he finished up one of the biggest gangsters in Melbourne, and he was shot dead).

The boys weren't allowed in the girls' yard, it was a serious thing, but some boys were fair little devils who'd get across, and then they'd open the door of your lavatory closet while you were in there, to see if you were doing your clothes up or down. They used to fight and stick their pen nibs in you. One day they gave me a present, and I unwrapped it to find a tobacco tin full of a whole heap of live cockroaches. And when they were sitting behind me in the classroom, they'd get my great big long plait and dig the curl on the end in a china inkwell, and it might be red ink or purple ink or blue ink or whatever ink. At last the teacher caught them and thrashed them with her cane — the teacher had a hell of a go, and she was a maiden lady who played the violin.

Then it was the day I sneaked my hand-sewing home, and Mum sewed up my French seams; but the teacher said they were done wrong and I had to unpick them. Mum was an expert sewer and she was that cross she got dressed up and went down to the school and told that teacher off. Mum said when she wanted the likes of her to show her anything it'd be coming to something.

When it was the school picnic at Henley Beach, I put green leaves inside my sunhat like Mum said, so I wouldn't get sunstruck, but I forgot about my legs and feet. They went turkey-red, and I kept going in the sea and coming out, and going in again to try and cool them down. But the salt water gave me prickly heat, and then the sun burnt the salt into my body and the pain was wicked, and by the time I got home my legs were three times the size they should have been, and my feet were like balloons. I couldn't walk and Mum had to put my feet up on pillows, because if the blood went down, your eyes would get affected. I was in bed for three weeks with sunbeam paralysis.

I got the red measles from that school, and it was like someone had stung me all over with pins. And because some kids had lice, Mum was always combing my hair with a fine comb and she got sick of it. So she went round to St Joseph's, the nuns' school in Russell Street, and asked if they had room for one more little girl who wasn't a Catholic, but a good girl.

I never went back to the Gilles Street School again. From then on I had a lot of happy school times with the nuns of St Joseph's, who taught respectable things. It was a very hard school to go to, and if you weren't a special sort of person you weren't allowed to go to that school in the first place.

I played the piano for the kids to march into school, and you had to write nicely and do proper spelling and do your grammar, and if we were singing we had to have the right notes. Everything was done as it was written, and we had cooking lessons and household days, and the nuns taught us pie-crust making, and how to do stews and roast dinners and sandwiches and supper things. When we had school in another language we had to translate it from theirs into England or vice versa. We did arithmetic where we had to turn it over or put it back, and physical geography; and I was good at skippy and could toe dance and do acrobatics and hang upside down. And I did fancy lace mats and music and painting and elocution and algebra and heaven knows what. I even learnt to do Latin and Spanish at St Joseph's, so I could read the Catholic Church books as if I was a Catholic.

The nuns weren't nasty or anything, but you had to be well-behaved to be in with them or they'd whack you with a cane or a long ruler that had every number on it. They didn't rouse at you for nothing, and you had to behave yourself a lot. If you came with dirty shoes you'd get put out the front — you had to be pretty tidy in that Catholic school. I had a bit of a thing for talking when you weren't supposed to, and if they caught me I'd have to go and kneel on the steps of the altar with a Bible on my head for a quarter of an hour.

Sister St Patrick was the head nun, and she was a tall lady, but not huge, dressed in her long thing with white all round her, and she was particular what you did, you had to be exactly right to please her. Sister Di Rossi was small with a hooked nose, and she was a nobleman's daughter from overseas in Italy, or wherever they came from, with a wonderful turn for figures — she'd put a sum yards long on the blackboard and run her finger up all the columns at once and get the answer. Another nun's name was Nazimova . . . or was that the actress in original moving pictures who kissed Rudolph Valentino before dying in the camellias?

Before we started school in the morning we had to learn something out of the Bible. When school finished for the day all the Catholic kids had to say their prayers, but they didn't look down on me beause I wasn't a Catholic, and I was allowed to quietly get out and go home.

The nuns made rosary beads of pearls and crystals and all the rest of it, and strung silver and gold chains with Jesus on the cross. When you got marked very high in your schoolwork for doing some Catholic subject about something long ago, they'd give you a holy necklace for the prize. I won a stack of them, and one string of rosary beads was a beauty: each bead was carved from ivory in the shape of a rose, and it was sent out in a shiny box by a big bloke from Ireland, and I won it, and you could loop it round your neck a few times, and it was worth goodness knows what. And then the

Pope of Rome sent out a prize from Italy, and every child in the school went in for this examination of past times, and I was about the only Protestant kid in the school but I did the best history of the Catholic religion, and the Pope gave the prize, and I won it. I got the first prize, and it was a silver thing like a carriage that you rolled your serviette up in: it was a silver serviette ring presented by the Pope of Rome to the top one, and the Catholics didn't get it but I got it. I don't like bragging, but somehow you can sort of do it and win all the best prizes if you're made that way.

There are some people that, right from the start, know what no one else can see through, even – like me and my way of knowing things. It's in your body and it comes from the adenoids. You're born with whatever you're mixed up with, and the adenoids are little tiny things in your blood vessels and your other parts, and somehow they bring you out into the finish of the bigger thing. We don't know how we work at all, really. The world's a very mixed up sort of a place. Everything that comes: the people, the animals, the birds . . . they all grow their own kind of pattern, on account of the adenoids.

German people are very sedate in not talking about things that are not too nice. Mum didn't tell me anything – she just gave me an elastic belt with a sort of bandage folded in on safety-pins that she'd got from a nurse who'd been going round where people had young girls, just in case, on my behalf. So that was the first bandage thing I ever wore and I had to keep on wearing one – I even had to go to school with a bandage on. Then after a while it went away; then after a while it started again.

Not far from St Joseph's was a big brick building that had been there for ages, before Adelaide was built almost. One end of it was a factory for the chemistry of making soap, and down the other end the manufacturers from years ago used the hair from lovely ladies to make wigs and long plaits, and lots of well-to-do parents bought curls for when their kids went dancing.

Everyone hated the soap factory, because on boiling-down days sooty black stuff would come over everything and ruin your washing if it was on the line. Mum and the other ladies round about kept putting up petitions to have the soap people put out.

There were barrels of fat in the soap factory, and one night some silly arse must have gone home and left something burning, because people saw smoke coming out the windows, and then the whole factory was on fire. It was night-time and there were flames and a roaring noise, and things were going crash and everyone was frightened, and people were running from all over to watch the soap factory fall down and make a bonfire.

And then we couldn't go to school for days, because St Joseph's was covered in black soot from the burning fats and oils and soap scents, and the wigs and plaits and all the other stuff.

As for the way the weather changes, it's different now. It's like the things were when they were only made from nothing – when they reckon Jesus made all the different things and they were done then like we do them now. Because even the plants and animals are coming on differently now; and everything's got a kind of a religious atmosphere at the back of it, as in the old times. And last week and the week before there were two huge thunder-storms of frozen ice-blocks that broke down lots of houses. It was just like pieces of stone coming out of the sky and it hadn't been seen for I don't know how long ago – since the whole of the area up above the world turned into frozen asset. It's the kind of weather we haven't had for hundreds of years. It's something to do between the moon and the stars up the sky, where the hot ones are melting the others and making them leave go where they usually stay.

Mum got sick of the cheeky bitch next door and the drunk men from the pub and the cars in the back yard and the boiling-down days at the new soap factory, so Dad supervised the building of a house in Honeychurch Avenue, North Unley. It was built from stone chipped by a proper stonemason, and had jarrah floors and polished woodwork and carvings all round the fireplaces; and Mum had everything put how she wanted it. North Unley was a select neighbourhood of fussy people who were very particular on the way their neighbours lived.

Uncle Alex had gone up the country to work and Uncle Egbert had switched to daytime driving, so they didn't shift with us. Dad had double the number of cars he'd started off with, and now he let his drivers take them to their own homes after work. The only car Dad brought to Honeychurch Avenue to use privately for himself was the royal blue one he drove the famous people of Adelaide about in.

Most other Unley people had a horse and trap, and lots of the ones with big families of children had a cow walking round their back yard, eating all their plants. A chap from Cherry Gardens would collect the cows after they'd been milked in the morning, and take them right up to the Long Paddocks at Kingswood. He always had a sulphur-crested cockatoo on his shoulder, and he'd go along whistling like mad and cracking his stockwhip; and in the afternoon he'd bring the cows home. We got our milk from Granny Treloar, a little wrinkled old woman with a face like a turkey gobbler, who had a dairy in Queen Street, and it had lovely cream on it when you scalded it gently. After Hopedene Street, it was like being in the country. Across from St Augustine's church was a liquorice-root paddock, where all the Unley kids went for a chew. By the school was a paddock with prickly bushes that were always full of goldfinches, and a man used to cut a track through the prickles and creep along with a net so he could catch the birds to sell.

Our new garage was up high, because the land to one side of it sloped down to a deep creek that started off up in the Hills where people went for picnics under the gum trees. I'd wade up in the creek odd times with a bit of steak on a string and catch yabbies; sometimes I'd paddle along in a canoe. When it rained heavily the creek filled up and came nearly into our back yard.

The man who lived across the other side of the creek was high up in the Military, and very spruce, with his leggings and belt and brass just so. But he carried it off at home the same as he did in the Military, and he was that strict his nickname was Tiger. His kids went in fear of his leather riding crop, and he had a girl a bit younger than me called Frizz, because of her hair, who used to cop all the hidings. And Tiger was an amateur gardener who went in for the carnation shows, and he'd make little paper collars for his prize exhibits and slide them up under the petals, then get a pair of tweezers and arrange each petal all round; and he had a fern-house with twenty-seven elkhorns, and a special shed full of tubs for his liquid manure. He was a great one for manure, and Frizz would be out in the street every day with a shovel, collecting; and he'd send her down to the parklands with a cart to collect the cowpats. And she had to bring back sand from the creek, and she was always in the carnation garden, weeding and watering. But North Unley had a very poor service for water and Frizz would be out there summer night-times, holding the hose, with just a trickle coming out, and she had a terrific big garden to water.

Dad dug a well in the yard to fit in the pump of a windmill, so Mum just had to turn the tap on to have her own water from underground for the garden. And we had a rain-water tank on a stand and a pond with water-lilies; and Dad planted fruit trees, a pepper tree, a grape arbour, and stuck down a new china frog on the front verandah, and made a copy of St Augustine's out of seashells for the middle of the front lawn. Mum had barrels with holes in the sides, and when her strawberries grew, they poked out. She kept digging up the garden so she could put in more dahlias and once Honeychurch Avenue had been part of the Chinese Gardens, where Chinamen grew vegetables, so she often dug up Chinese coins.

Mum kept black fowls that were thoroughbreds, with a purply shadowy sort of wave through their blackness; there was a private house for when the hens were sitting, so nothing could worry them. The big white rooster would go you if you touched one of his tribe – those father chooks were jealous, they reckoned the lady chooks were theirs. You had to be careful when you went to get the eggs, or that rooster might take a piece of meat out of you. We had hundreds of blooming things – we had turkeys and all, and Mum got a fair bit when she sold her turkeys at Christmas, or when people were having a dinner party or a wedding, and wanted one to make the meal.

When Mum got some Rhode Island Red fowls with ginger feathers that laid big pale pinky-golden eggs, the man next door was always leaning over the fence asking me if they'd been laying, and wanting to swap some of their eggs for his peaches. If I did, he'd bump each egg in turn against his bottom teeth to crack it, and tip the raw egg down his throat. And even if his own hens had only laid a couple, he'd tip the raw egg down his throat and tell his wife they hadn't been laying, and that'd really make the old girl wild.

Mum started sneaking down and counting the eggs in the fowlhouse, and got on to the fact that I was giving them away. She marched in next door and went crook, and the old girl went crook back at Mum for rousing about her husband.

But Mum and the people next door were soon friends again. The man who ate the eggs had a kiosk like a little house on the corner of Grote Street that sold magazines and papers, and he gave Mum some fancywork magazines full of good stuff; and Mum gave him a pot of her fig and preserved ginger jam; and then he gave Mum a duck egg over the fence.

Mum had room for one more egg under a broody hen, so she put the duck egg in with the ordinary eggs, and when that duck chicken came out it was a pretty furry little thing like a toy. The hen was so proud, till the duck chicken made straight for the lily pond, and then she nearly went mad: she was squawking and flapping her wings because her chicks shouldn't swim.

The old rooster seemed to know right from the start that it wasn't one of his tribe, and he kept trying to peck the duck chicken. While Mum went to get a cage to put it away by itself, she handed it to me, and the little thing sat in my hand. And from that very day on it never left me.

He was a gander Muscovy duck chicken and I named him Deedle because there was something belonging to the sound of his breed that sounded "Deedle" to me. He was voracious for green stuff, and I fed him on cabbages and lawn clippings and weeds. He grew into a long white shopper duck with proper duck feet and a yellow beak, but he didn't ever bite me because he was my own tame Muscovy duck that was more like a pet cat.

If Deedle saw me coming out the back door he'd wait for me, and if I whistled or called he'd come flapping up to see me. He went everywhere with me in the yard, and if I sat down he'd want me to lift him up. He'd sit on my lap, and I'd rock him with my knees and nurse him and pat him and sing to him, and if I put his head under one of his wings he'd go fast asleep, and I could put him down anywhere and he'd stay there, asleep.

But Deedle didn't like strangers much, and he particularly disliked men. If a man went to pat Deedle, he'd bite them: Deedle had a favourite fantasy for male persons. And ladies were naturally frightened of him, and Mum wore grey stockings and it seemed Deedle couldn't bear the colour grey. Mum couldn't even go out to get some water from the tank in her stockings: if Deedle was about he'd go for her. Mum hated Deedle.

One afternoon when I came home from school, I couldn't find Deedle anywhere. Mum acted a bit funny when I asked her about him, and then when Dad said he was looking forward to a nice tender duck properly stuffed up with herbage and bacon for his dinner, I knew he meant Deedle.

I didn't have any dinner that night, I just cried. And I told Mum and Dad they were cannibals to eat poor Deedle like that.

A lot of high-up places in the mountains where the snow comes haven't been like it for hundreds of years. The sun melts that ice up there and gets it going a lot and that brings it down on the moon and the moon lights it up some more,and then we get it on the earth. The ground's going rotten underneath because a lot of the big trees are eating all the moisture out of the earth, and the soil is getting too crumbly so the houses are moving and big cracks are opening up in the walls that you can put your hand into. Big pieces of the ground are falling in and revealing deep trenches and caves and big floods of water that they didn't even know were there. It's Armageddon — the whole nature of the earth is turning over from one place to the other. The world's not like it ought to be. It's weird. They say we don't know half of what's going on.

I was a prodigy of learning, and the nuns of St Joseph's could only teach a kid so much, and by the time I was into the teen ages I knew just about everything they knew. So then I left school and had to go for messages, and help Mum with the housework and the garden. And I practised my drawing, and I could do a drawing with a pencil that'd be better than the thing you did with the camera. And I practised my music on an original piano from Berlin that had real ivory keys and carved brass handles and candlesticks that opened out when you pulled them. When you had a piano, little kids came sometimes, and they might get to something, so after I'd finished playing I'd lock the keyboard. On hot summer nights, all the people in Honeychurch Avenue would be out on their verandahs in deck-chairs, and I'd open the front room windows and play all my prettiest piano pieces – Mum and Dad, and the people next door, and the people across the road would be listening, and appreciating my playing.

And I played the piano while they sang the hymns in Sunday School and I taught Bible history about how the spirits in the sky came, and how the sacred ones could come from little children; and about the one that came down on his own and found the girl, Eve, and then when Baby Jesus came it all went back to Egypt where the pyramids were. I must have had two heads in my youth, I reckon, because I knew so much.

Then I started riding my bike right down past the parklands and way out to Norwood a couple of days a week (I'd been riding a bike from the day I got out of the cradle, nearly). That bike I rode was a beauty – it was a silver-grey and had nice fittings and pedals, and a bell and night-lights and all. I was riding such a long distance to a high Catholic convent to learn special advanced drawing and painting and piano and singing because I was a bit beyond the ordinary.

The convent was a big Catholic turn-out, a real top Christian place, where the young nuns were given their veils and went through the ceremony of being a virgin. One day the music-teacher nun showed me through the chapel, and after you went up the steps to get in the atmosphere was uncanny. There were huge paintings in hand-carved wood frames on the walls from their religion, and it seemed like any of the people in the paintings could come out and say Hello. And the statue of the Virgin Mary with the Baby in her arms looked that real, too, you could've talked to it; and I saw all the objects belonging to their ceremonies from the holy water things to the big candle they gave them on the day they became a nun, and it was supposed to be their life and it was alight when they gave it to them and when they died that candle got blown out – it was part of the ceremony.

The music-teacher nun taught me good proper piano playing and I could play just as naturally as I'd tap a table, and I did cross hands and continental fingering and wrist attacks and triplets and trilly ones and vibrations and half-notes and animated basses and presto with finger leaps. I could get the piano to sound like an orchestra and shake my head the right way, as if it was out in a breeze, and sing "Beautiful Star of Heaven" at the exact same time I played "Melody of Peace". When I passed my big piano exam I got a medal with my initials on it that I wore on a chain round my neck.

Singing was a pretty complicated business with a lot of weird things – it was marvellous how I could do it, but it wasn't easy. I learnt scales singing up and down to get a certain tone; I got a certificate for Transposition; I learnt the theory of it all and the timing. I gargled my voice in oil and didn't eat things that were too bitey: vinegar would screw up your neck; lemons and oranges and pineapples were a very vivid kind of fruit that would burn up your lungs; fish or meat with salt in it gave you a nasty cough and affected your eyes. I had a high contralto voice and a far-ahead talent to be a better singer, and the music-teacher nun gave me different words to songs that she didn't generally give to others. If she had a nice young visiting gentleman, she'd put us two on the stage and we'd mix it up into a duet. We'd sing "Roses of the South" and "Thora", but I wasn't a forward sort of girl, and some of the gentlemen would put me on edge if they looked at me and grinned.

Mum had Blackboy roses growing on the back fence, and I painted them in my art lessons with very fine brushwork. And I did pears and plums growing in Mum's fruit garden, and grapes growing on Mum's vines, and Mary Pickford with sausage curls, and a cathedral at sunset. And I painted a statue of a naked man, but men had a queer set-up there, really, so I painted in a fig leaf because I didn't go in for eerie subjects as a rule.

I was a born artist, and I'd come home and draw things – even elephants and everything. If I saw a person with beautiful eyes sometimes, when I was travelling on my bike, I'd remember them, and if I drew a pretty face I'd put those eyes in. Because a lot of people had a nice face, but they didn't have nice eyes – their eyes looked hard or too funny.

But one day riding my bike, looking at eyes, I ran over a stone and fell off, and when I fell I hit my face on the handlebars and two big bottom teeth smashed off in the gum. I went to a dentist at Glenelg, because that was a clever place for making new teeth. He put me to sleep, and when I woke up I had a raw place where my teeth used to be. I got two new false front teeth which looked just like my own, but I had to often take them out and scrub them with a brush. It's nasty when your teeth get broken by accident, because I had lovely teeth to start with. They weren't too big or too small; they went together very nicely.

When I had my sixteenth birthday, Mum thought I was old enough to go on a holiday by myself, so I got booked in on a ship to visit Aunty Eva over in Western Australia. There was only just one place empty for one more private person, because the ship was full with hundreds of Tasmanian soldiers going off to the War. Mum gave the head stewardess extra money to keep me away from the boys, and said I was a good girl and that I knew all they knew that I knew, and wasn't the sort of girl who'd get behind somewhere quiet and not be seen. So I got my bunk on the ship that no one else could have.

Though I wasn't seasick, all the big ships carried coconuts to give to the people who were. If you cracked the coconut and drank the juice it would cure the worst bout of seasickness in half an hour, and you might drink it out of the shell if you wished.

I wasn't allowed to go past a certain part of the high deck where the soldiers were, and the soldiers weren't allowed to encroach on the private property of the people who'd bought their fare to go to Western Australia. But they used to whistle to me and try to get me up there; they thought I was so pretty, and because of my golden hair I was like a big doll; and not being with any girls while they were in the Army waiting to go on over to Egypt, and then to France to fight, they wanted me to come up with them. But I wasn't permitted, though they kept throwing threepences and sixpences and once a half-crown at me. The head stewardess wouldn't let me keep the soldiers' money – she took it away and put it in a Santa Claus Society envelope to keep for the poor children who had empty money-boxes.

Aunty Eva was waiting on the wharf and she told me she took packets of the Holy Gospels everywhere she travelled – by land or by water – and left them to be found under seat cushions. She smelt of cedar on Sundays because she kept her best black silk dress wrapped in tissue paper in a cedar chest, and her best hat, too, and took them out to wear to church. And she wore them on the weekday her canary died, and he lay in state till sundown in a Huntley and Palmer's biscuit tin, and then was buried under a rose bush in the back garden.

I thought I'd stay in Western Australia for months, but I only stayed a week. My cousin, Violet, was a morbid child who liked to eat tea-leaves and had a nervous trick of sniffing. She was ten years old and she wasn't a friendly child, and if she couldn't have her own way she'd cry and reckon I'd made her miserable and start having one of her bilious attacks. She'd tear the clothes off her dolls and smash their faces and say I'd done it. In the middle of the night she'd creep down to the laundry with a blanket and put it under the tap; next thing she'd be in bed again, crying and yelling that I'd been up in the night and wet her bed-clothes. And I couldn't stay there any more after Violet got taken with even worse mischievous inclinations and tried to cut off my eyebrows when I was asleep.

I learnt off everybody that was the highest one in Australia, really, and after I'd learnt all I could from the nuns at the convent, I went to learn painting from Miss Madge Homewood – an old style English-lady artist, a lady of the old school through and through. She never married in her life, and always wore silver-grey dresses that toned in with her hair and old-fashioned shady hats trimmed with pansies and wistaria. She lived in a street down behind us near the parklands, with her sisters, Miss Ettie and Miss Flo, the instrumentalists, and their father, Mr Homewood, the professor of music. Homewoods had a big orchestra of their own where they all sang; and Miss Madge had a studio in one of the tall buildings in town where she taught art to ladies; and Miss Ettie and Miss Flo had a music school above.

Miss Madge's studio was an enormous room, nearly made of glass, and some of the ladies were high-class socialites, and you could do oil painting or water-colour painting or china painting. I had a polished wooden palette and a lot of different apparatus that I put in a box and locked, so no one could pinch my best brush or any nice foreign-brand pencil I might have. Miss Madge handed round cups of tea while you worked, and all day you heard the instruments practising upstairs.

The china painters were up one end doing their snowdrops and daffodils and ox-eye daisies; us oil and water-colour painters were down the other. You could bring in pictures to copy, or paint what Miss Madge posed, but I'd started wanting to do originals out of my head. It must have been the adenoids, because a picture just came to me, and if it was a worthwhile picture I painted it.

One particular painting I did was called "The Pearls of the Sea", and it was so good I've never got over it. There was a boat that came in from overseas and it ran into the rocks and it was sinking, and the man that was the master of it was looking over the side at this lady who was supposed to be a mermaid, and she'd come out of the sea and was holding her hands up to him, and she didn't have any clothes on, and she had these pearls round her neck, all hanging, and her long hair down her back. The sea was waving up behind and the boat looked like it was flapping, and it was wonderful, and it was me who'd done it, and Mum hung it in the passage but some devil pinched it.

"The Prisoner" was a real lady, who came from a gymnasium place in Melbourne where they taught girls to get good figures, and she had double-jointed wrists and ankles and everything; she sat for us as a model with no clothes on and just a chain round each wrist, but you couldn't see anything of her much because of her long hair. "Departing" was Bertie Quigley going to be a soldier on a horse and black teardrops like watermelon seeds came out of the sky, and a horse looking at you was one of the worst things you could paint. And I painted a picture of the ladies from the royal palace in the dresses with the low necks and there were grape-vines with the grapes coming down and the ladies singing and they had the cherry-blossom Jap lanterns and it went into rainbow-autumn colours: all the lanterns and the grapes and ladies' faces looking up. And I sat in front of a mirror and watched myself and painted a replica of my looks, and I was really surprised how lovely it came out. And I even painted the Bavarian Mountains, the land that Granma and Granpa Hoff and Adam and Eve came from when the world first came to earth. Up there was the city of peace, and there was snow like a heap of frozen ice puddings, and great dips so deep you'd have to mind where you were going or you'd go to billyoh down them, and tunnels where if you went in you'd never get out again. I did it all with little brushes that only had about three hairs, and I put in the Tree of Paradise that had ripe fruit like raspberries, and Jesus was up on the cross at the side. It was amazing, but Miss Madge thought it weird.

Once I posed for Miss Madge's ladies with a lace camisole on. My arms were bare, and you could see the skin on my back through the lace. I was sitting in front of a mirror, looking at myself, and I had a hairbrush in my hand and was supposed to be doing my hair.

Another time Miss Madge painted me as the model all for herself. I wore my blue costume and my pink frilly blouse stitched with a gold colour little thread; and I had my long golden hair and a blue hat with an ostrich feather that hung over like a fringe (I used to wear a lot of blue because it suited my eyes). And Miss Madge painted me and called it "The Bridesmaid" and they put it in the Art Gallery: I was hung up in a gold frame for everyone to see.

Lots of people who had a boy killed in the War would bring his photograph to Miss Madge, and she'd do them a painting of their lost soldier-boy half life-size and charge them very reasonable. The photos were always of boys in full uniform with nice faces, and some stood on their front verandah before they went to the War. When Miss Madge was doing a painting from a photo it would make you want to cry.

Last week there was a big star scramble – a scramble of some big stars that were coming down out of the top of the sky. Some weighed the others down and made them too heavy, and they didn't have enough gas from the atmosphere to hold them up, and they came down on a beach somewhere. I went out to look because I couldn't go to sleep. I saw them coming down from the sky and it hurt your eyes, nearly, to watch. The fire in the sky gradually went up and up and up, and big stars and other things were shooting through the top, and then they were dropping down and crashing. It was absolutely some horrible thing that was caused by the electricity in the redness of the earth.

Though Mum was descended from the Bavarian Mountains, she was a great one for Our Boys in the War. When we lived in Hopedene Street she made a monster Australian flag and flew it from a pole by the front gate every time the soldiers marched past. One day a general wanted that flag, so Mum let him have it to take to the War. And Mum rolled bandages and knitted khaki things and sent off Christmas puddings all year round, and she had to pay ever so much to send them.

But when the War was over, Mum went back to being stuck-uppified and above everybody and German again. She reckoned you couldn't hardly look over the front fence of a night without getting your head knocked off, with all the returned soldiers roaming about: they were that cheeky, and they passed remarks and put some words in you'd never heard before. Mum was very careful about what I did any listening to, or accidentally found out, but I knew the soldiers in the Army had a bad name because they'd been in strange countries on bits of leave from duty, and of course, being natural people, they couldn't stay away from the girls. And a lot of them went with the girls that weren't any good for them, like the wild desert women that lived in the tents (and you could even pick up very funny things from the ladies in London and France, who were more far ahead in certain ways than we believed in).

It was a pretty touchy time and girls had to be careful. Mum was very particular about people not letting some of their looks go outside their clothes, and was disgusted at how many proper-looking girls were going out practically half-undressed, or anything. Mum said it wasn't safe for a girl to go out when she was all dressed up, even.

But Bertie Quigley was still a real gentlemanly sort of boy in the old-fashioned style when he came home from the War; and he had brown curly hair and big brown eyes, and was strong and well-built. Bertie had got some nasty bumps and broken bones in the War, but he went back to his old job of doing woodwork and carpentry at a furniture factory, and he made me a little toy cabinet with drawers to put my veils and gloves in.

And Bertie was a good sport and could make you laugh if he liked, and he kept riding his push-bike over to North Unley to see me. He took me to visit his mother and father, and we went to his aunty and uncle's for tea on a Sunday night; and Bertie never brought me home late, and sometimes he'd bring me a box of chocolates. When we went to girls' birthday parties Bertie wouldn't think of sitting at the table first if there were ladies around – he'd push your chair in nicely.

If it was a fine day we'd go for a walk, or to the Unley Oval to watch the football. Night-times the Oval turned into an open-air picture theatre with a screen rigged up on the grass and a lady playing the piano. Bertie and I would sit out there with our rugs and pillows, and often we'd see Tiger from across the other side of the creek watching the pictures with his wife. Frizz was supposed to stay home and look after her little sister, but as soon as Tiger and her mum had gone, she'd bundle the kid into a pram and push her down to the street by the Oval. Then she'd park the pram and shin up a tree and watch the pictures through the leaves. She'd have to miss out on the end and rush to get home before Tiger and her mum.

Mr Quigley used to say if Bertie never got anyone worse than me he'd be damn lucky, but, though I liked Bertie a lot, I never felt he belonged to me: we were just friends. I wasn't a kissy person, I couldn't be bothered with sloppies, so I only let Bertie kiss me on the cheek. He said I ought to be living in Russia where he'd heard it was unlawful to give kisses in public, even to your mother – he said fines were being inflicted on those who practised osculations in the street, or in railway trains or tramcars; and you could also be fined if you put kisses on a postcard.

Mum and Dad wouldn't let me go with just anybody, and they knew Bertie was decent, but they wanted me to find somebody up higher: they didn't think Bertie was good enough. Quigleys had been all right when I'd been a kid, and Mrs Quigley did the washing and ironing and cooking and took me to pantomimes. Mrs Quigley had seemed, then, like a lady, but now I was seeing Bertie, Mum didn't like her. Mum talked about Mrs Quigley as if she was just a washerwoman from the back streets of Adelaide with a certain ancient religion that had as funny ways of doing things as the Salvation Army. And if anything to do with your gas went bung, Mr Quigley could fix it, but Dad didn't think it much of a job for a man to do, and he didn't think much of carpenters, even though he smoked up all the special cigars Bertie had brought him back from overseas.

I was a tall girl, fairly well-built, though I never was fat – I wasn't a real pudding like some girls you saw. I had violetty-blue eyes with dark lashes and skin like silk and rosy cheeks, and if I got warm my face went even pinker. So I never used powder or anything like that, and I didn't need lipstick because if you had plenty of blood you had colour in your lips and gums and everywhere.

In summer I went out with a sun-umbrella and a hat, and I knew a girl who was a milliner at Miller Anderson's in Hindley Street, and she taught me to make any kind of hat and trim it. I had a hat with a silk rose, a hat with wax strawberries, a hat with velvet geraniums, a hat with fluffy fur pompoms, the hat with the ostrich feather I wore for Miss Madge . . . some hats fitted my head, some came down at the side, several were shaped like beehives: I had as many as seventeen hats at a time, big and small, and one was an exact copy of one of Queen Mary's hats.

Sometimes I wore my gold hair up, waved and puffed and twisted, sometimes I wore it hanging down with a butterfly bow; and I could sit on it, and it was such fine hair the hairpins slipped out as fast as I put them in. I wore my hair down when the chemist who lived across from us in Honeychurch Avenue wanted to try out his new camera, and Mum let me sit for him. And I had on my cream crepe de chine blouse with black ribbon-velvet stripes, and the brooch at my collar was the family brooch that Granpa Rodda gave to Granma Rodda, and then she gave it to me. It was a brooch made from a piece of the rock, volcanic and crystallised, from that Mount Etna that sunk in the subterranean thing hundreds of years ago, when the whole city went down under the sea. It was a cameo brooch carved with a lady's face, and she had a bunch of grapes on her head. Two ear-rings went with it that dingle-dangled in your ears, but I couldn't put them in mine: my ears were too fatty, and it hurt if I screwed things on. And I couldn't wear a wrist watch because I had too much electricity in my body – Aunty Eva sent me a watch, once, but before I'd finished doing up its strap it had stopped.

My aunties were kind, and I got a lot of nice things from them when they went away for holidays to the Islands or overseas. Aunty Albertina gave me a ring with Indian rubies and a necklace of pearls that came out of the sea (they weren't the homemade pearls, but the ones that had a big history and came out of the shells). Aunty Rose gave me a shawl from France all done with silver in it, to wear with a low neck. I got lace collars and lace scarves, and some elegant underclothes with embroidered dots, scallops and daisy sprays.

Mum was a clever sewer, treadling her Singer sewing-machine, and she made silk dance dresses with frills you could have gone to your wedding in. I went to a fancy-dress turn-out in one of them, and I was like Cinderella in my long white dress: like a beautiful queen: like the Queen of the Fairies. And I had high-heeled shoes and long gloves, and I was supposed to be an angel, and I had a pair of gold wings on my back and a crown of flowers round my head, because I was the Queen of the Angels with my golden fair hair hanging down.

When it was the ball in the Unley Town Hall to celebrate the end of the War, Mum cut me out an old-fashioned dress of cream satin and sewed it into the dress the lady wore on the Peace Loan badge. Everybody knew that lady, and when I wore the dress and held up the flag, my sleeve hung down like a curtain and on it was the ensign thing with the shield and the wattle and the boomerang the blackies threw: Mum had cut them out of satin and I'd helped her stitch them on by hand, and then we'd stitched on PEACE LOAN FOR THE SOLDIERS.

Bert Quigley was my partner in a special Army uniform from being a very high Anzac who'd been to the mountains. He had his medals and stripes and his rifle, and he was the soldier who was guarding us women, and yet I was the sainted lady on the Peace Loan badge who guided him when he was fighting and protected him from getting done – they reckoned God loaned the angel to guard the soldier that was good, so he wouldn't get killed.

It was a wonderful show, and when it was time for the judging, Bertie had his rifle on his shoulder, and the band played as we marched round the dance room with the others in costume. There were hundreds to choose from, but Peace Loan for the Soldiers was named the best-costumed pair for the whole ball.

Bertie and I had our photo taken and then went up on the stage to get our prizes. Bertie got a cheque and I got a bath-heater you put the chips in, and it was exactly what Mum and Dad wanted.

It was black as ink outside last night, you couldn't hardly see at all. There was a funny looking moon with smudges over it; and there're funny moons, and I don't know what, up there because a lot of queer stuff's coming down from the heavens that we haven't seen for hundreds of years. The earth's bringing everything down, and all those aeroplanes with their petrol burning are causing so much vapour in the air that it's making the stars move, because they don't like that vapour apparently, and they're coming down to get cool.

One day a soldier called Arnold Bywaters rang up to say he was sorry to be an intrusion, but he thought he'd left his pyjama-suit in one of Dad's cars. So Dad searched round till he found a small parcel, and left a message at the Army camp, and Arnold Bywaters got into a row for sneaking out without leave.

The next day I opened the front door to a soldier in uniform, and that was when I first met Arnold Bywaters. He was a squarish-built type from the country, pretty muscly and tidy, with tiny black curls all over his head. Dad gave him the pyjamas, and a little drink of very good wine to wish him luck. Arnold Bywaters said he was an orphan, with only an aunty for a relation in Adelaide, and could he come and see us again. Mum and Dad thought he was a decent, nicely spoken chap, an older-natured person, more sensible than most soldiers, and after that Arnold Bywaters was always round at Honeychurch Avenue, drinking Dad's wine or having afternoon tea. When he was discharged from the Army to go back to his big farm up at Central Eyre's Peninsula, he used to write and sometimes he'd come down on leave from the animal business to see us.

Arnold Bywaters was a real toff in his civvies – he was so fussy in his gentleman's white collar and navy blue suit, you'd have thought he'd come from Government House. He brought Mum sides of mutton and sheepskin rugs, and was handy if Dad was doing anything with the car. Mum kept saying how Arnold Bywaters, with his farm and his thoroughbred cows and sheep, was a millionaire, just about – and he was bachelorised off by himself because he didn't seem to have a girlfriend, and he wasn't cheeky or a swearer or a smoker, and perhaps if I behaved myself he might be a good friend. Arnold Bywaters listened to my singing and admired my painting and – I couldn't understand it really, but, without meaning to – I went to the pictures with him; and he started coming round in a white suit, white socks and a white yachting cap to take me rowing on the River Torrens; and I got to know Arnold Bywaters a lot, quite a bit, for a long time.

I was never that way inclined to be looking out to get married like some girls that were so anxious – I wasn't keen on marrying anybody. I wasn't a kissy sort. I didn't like being hugged or kissed or anything much, and Arnold Bywaters wasn't a very huggy person either. I didn't know whether I liked him or whether I didn't. But I was supposed to be engaged to him because he'd given me a ring of opals and diamonds (though Mum didn't think opals were lucky). Then Arnold Bywaters took me out to see his aunty, who said she was very pleased with what he'd chosen to have.

Arnold Bywaters went back up the country and started building me a beautiful house that was to be nearly a duplicate of Mum and Dad's, only bigger, so I wouldn't feel strange and at a loss for home. He kept writing and asking did I want a nursery; did I want a bakehouse; did I want fireplaces in all the rooms; was there anything I'd like to have he hadn't thought of.

Then Arnold Bywaters wanted me to come up to see the house he was building. But he lived on his farm by himself and Mum and Dad didn't like me going away up to Central Eyre's Peninsula to be on my own with him, because they didn't want a bad name.

Mum and Dad had a bit of a talk with each other. Mum said she thought Arnold Bywaters had been brought up pretty straight, and was a gentleman and honourable and if he had his bedroom and I had mine, they could trust him. Dad said a lot of people lived together and didn't start mucking round. So Arnold Bywaters came down to get me, and Mum and Dad spoke to him and said he'd better not do anything he shouldn't.

We went to Port Lincoln in a boat and Arnold Bywaters wore a straw hat with a cord at the side tied to his coat-button in case of a storm. We caught a train from there, two hundred miles inland, to a place full of snakes and lizards. He had prize sheep and prize cows, and a prize bull called Gallipoli, and a thoroughbred racehorse that stepped backwards and trod on my toe. There was just me and Arnold Bywaters together, but he was proper and never once came near my bedroom door.

He showed me the house he was building, and told me about chairs and tables and oak chests and crockery and saucepans and brass candlesticks and hearthrugs. He was much older than me and wanted everything done exactly right; he was very good in a way, but there was something about him that made me think how I was sick of being bossed round by Mum, and it seemed it was going to continue on from there. I'd never been keen on getting married in the first place; and it'd be a hard life for me, not being a farm girl; and he was too much of a grown-up man style; and he was jealous and got disgusted and started to argue every time I talked to any other fellow. All of a sudden I sort of knew I could never live in that place.

Mum and Dad thought it a shame when I came home; they kept rousing at me, but I wouldn't go back. When I stopped writing to Arnold Bywaters, he came down, very worried, to see what was going on. He asked if he'd done anything I didn't approve of, or was I interested in any other male person. He was upset and disappointed when I said I wasn't really terribly anxious to get married to anybody — getting married was a very messy business all round.

It's the atmosphere, you see — the aerial up above the world has changed its atmosphere. And the stars and all have changed; and the Hills up top look dirty sometimes — you can't see them hardly. And if that atmosphere comes down towards us too much, everyone will have to shift away. Even

when I went out early one morning, before six o'clock, the whole street was full of just like thick smoke – it was vapour, like a cold frost coming. It was those things in the sky melting and all the stuff coming down; and, as it comes down to the heat of the earth, it goes into smoke vapour. All the sky went into a big mist that morning, and I've never seen anything like it. I couldn't see my front fence from my front door: it was so thick, it might have been the middle of the night.

If I was out the front when the postman stopped at our letterbox he'd say something cheeky or laugh at me for being there with all my curls down my back. One day I was on the verandah in a new dress Mum had made, and I was spinning round to make the skirt float up, and just then the postman rode past on his bike and shouted that he could see things he shouldn't. The next day he saw me with a big red apple, and I was about to take a bite when he called, "Where's Adam?" So I threw the apple at him hard, and it was a dead shot: it hit him slap in the face and put him out of wobble and he fell off his bike, and the bike went down flat on its two wheels.

He went crook at me then, and said I had no right to be cruel to a postman delivering letters. I said a postman shouldn't yell at people while he was riding a push-bike on the footpath. We didn't speak for a while after that, but then it turned into a sort of joke, and he was as cheeky as ever.

One day I was playing the piano when the postman stopped at our letterbox, and he got off his bike and came right up on the verandah and tapped at the window. When I came out, he said I could play the piano nearly as good as he could play the violin. I thought he was joking, but he said if he came round after tea, could we play a duet. I asked Mum, who came to have a look at him, and he went very polite and gentlemanly and introduced himself as Stanley Hopps – though people called him Chooky. Mum thought if he was as serious about his music and as sensible as he appeared to be, it'd be all right; but if it turned out she didn't like him, that'd be it. So Chooky Hopps came round with his violin and we played together, and it was so good Mum and Dad didn't mind, though they didn't want him there every night.

His nickname was Chooky because he was his mother's youngest one, her chicken. He was an Anzac, an Original, who'd been at Gallipoli; he was the same age as Bertie Quigley. Because of the War he hardly had any hair left, so he wasn't that terribly good-looking. But he had a kind of golden-tan skin – though he wasn't a foreign man from overseas – and golden-grey eyes (Chooky said Queen Alexandra in London and lots of the other old royal family ladies had golden-grey eyes). He could play the piano and flute, but the violin was his masterpiece and he played on it like mad, his right arm as pliable as a swan's neck, and it was a nice violin, not a scratchy one: it was a sweet violin of a certain high make, and the strings were all silver and the hair in the bow was off some very famous animal; and sometimes for a trick Chooky would play it with his toes.

Chooky and I were clever musicians, and became partners in playing duets when there was a Saturday night dance at the Soldiers' Club; anything they could dance we could play, and we got supper and were paid for playing, too. When there was a big party or some Remembrance thing from the War we'd get requested to entertain, and often they'd give me a present like a teaset and Chooky, some article of clothing, to recompense us for what we did from our kindness. Chooky had a long flute that was hard to play because you needed a decent breath to blow, and usually we'd do our favourite duet, the piece that sounded like nightingales, and I'd sing over the notes and change from one key to another and know when to put the half-notes in between.

Sometimes when there was a dance on, Chooky took me for his partner; though there were some others I'd rather have danced with, because Chooky didn't like intricate dancing, and if he'd had a few drinks he got heavy on his feet. A lot of the other chaps reckoned I was a corker – I could swing, and whizz out on one foot and change, and come round with someone else (and if someone was eating lollies and dropped one, and you caught your heel in it, it was amazing how far you'd go). But once when it was the circular waltz where you changed partners, some silly arse spilt his beer, and I saw the little patch of wet on the floor – but you had to keep going, you couldn't stop when all the dancers were coming – and the nice-looking young man at the back of me slipped, and went right through my legs. It was done in an instant, and I sat on his belly and knocked every bit of wind out of him. Everyone laughed and I felt awful, but it was one of the funniest things going.

Gallipoli, where Chooky had been, was just about the most treacherous thing that ever happened in the War. Because those damn people were waiting up top and our boys had to come across from the beach, and they shot them as they came, and half our boys never got up again. Chooky had got knocked around a bit, and finished up in a hospital in England, where the nurses kept scratching his wounds so he wouldn't get sent to the front; but in the end they healed, and in France he had some bad shell-shock and gas business. It was an awful War and a lot far beyond them, and they went to places they'd never dreamt were there. Before

Gallipoli and England and France there'd been the pyramids and the wild women, and because of it all Chooky wasn't as good as he used to be. He could go very queer sometimes: he'd get tired and go to sleep, so if he took you out anywhere you'd be lucky to get home as he couldn't keep awake.

Chooky's father, Mr Hopps, was one of the heads of a big music warehouse in town that sold the king of all grand pianos, and he could take a piano worth thousands to pieces and put it together again. Chooky's mother, Mrs Hopps, was a nervous lady who preferred to wear red, and had a sort of very nice English accent without being too broad. She was pleased when Chooky took me down to meet her, because she'd worried he'd bring a foreign lady home from Egypt or somewhere; though she'd been hoping he'd behave himself and choose someone suitable. But Chooky's mother was a Catholic, though not terribly Catholicky, and wished I was a Catholic, too.

Dad didn't exactly pick Chooky up to nurse him, but he wasn't rude to him like Mum, who didn't think the Hopps family was as good socially as us. They lived in a little street in the part of Unley that wasn't flash; but the worst thing was that Chooky had once been a butcher in his uncle's shop at Beauville, and he wanted to go back to being that again. Butchers were bad enough, but Beauville was the place Mum and Dad had both come from – and was the place Mum wanted to forget. When she talked about Beauville you'd have thought the people who lived there came off the rubbish heap. When Chooky came to see me of a night, Mum had started acting as if she couldn't have anybody visiting if they weren't a Sir This, or the Lady Something Else, or what-not.

Chooky knew he couldn't face Mum if he was a butcher, and she didn't even like him much as a postman, so he tried to make himself respectable by getting a job in the tobacco shop on the corner of Rundle Street where they sold pipes and first-class cigarettes and cigars. He had nice suits and looked like a real gentleman, and wealthy people came in and wanted to buy things, and Chooky would sell them the right things, and they'd all come back again.

Mum was sedate and never told any dirty yarns, and Dad didn't either, but occasionally when Chooky told some funny story he might slip in something saucy. And if Mum tried to close the conversation, Chooky always had some little funny joke thing he'd say back. Mum still liked Arnold Bywaters. She said Arnold Bywaters was a grown-up man who would've been a good husband; but Chooky – even though he'd been to the War – was more like a cheeky boy.

Mum didn't like Chooky being so attentive to me – she thought he was too loveyfied altogether. Everyone had their own individuality, and Chooky had that certain atmosphere some men had with a girl. That type of man had it laid on – you could sort of read it, if he was sexy, though he mightn't even speak it out full. But that type had their own way of doing things (like a dog when it wanted to go with another dog): they had their way of communication.

And Mum didn't care for it. And she was tired of Chooky playing his violin; and he smoked cigarettes all the time, and it gave her the quince.

Adam and Eve were sort of made out of a recipe from the Lord, and he gave Adam an apple, though Adam wasn't supposed to give it to Eve, but Adam thought if he didn't give it to her he'd lose her, so she ate the apple that she said was the seed of life, and then he ate the apple and they became husband and wife, but they weren't really married – only by royal consent from the Lord. I think this Bible business is million of years beyond anything we ever knew. This world is just a little part of a place that started millions of years ago. It takes a long time for those funny star things to evolve, so they could have been there long before the world. And because people went up and walked on the moon there are things happening in the sky now that causes the sea to go mad; and different other things go queer, like we've never seen before.

I'd never had a rude thought about people's bodies, and for a long time I didn't understand what girls meant when I heard them talking about doing sexual this and that and something else. Once I asked Mum and she gave me a smack across the mug because she was a high class Lutheran, and Dad was a Methodist, and Granma and Granpa Hoff had come from the Bavarian Mountains and they were pretty strong religious people, those top class Germans.

I wasn't a lovey-dovey cat's-eye sort of person, I didn't like smooching, I never ever fancied sexy business with men. I never went with fellows and slept out with them, or went for picnics – I wasn't like that, I never was that sort of person. But some girls were dreadful – they let them pull their clothes down and all, but I would have slapped anyone's face if they'd tried. No, I wasn't like that; I'd been to the nuns and got trained.

But Mum found out by accident that Chooky was a bit of a doer with the girls, and said if he was doing any of that sort of thing with me she'd knock my head off. Next time Chooky came to the house, Mum told him to get out and said he wasn't to come poking his nose in where she didn't want him any more; Dad said if he was up to any of his tricks with me, he'd give him a good thumping.

But I didn't stop going out with Chooky because, anyhow, I'd just had my twenty-first birthday, and once you were past that you could adopt your own making-up of your mind. Mum and Dad were always rousing and going off pot at me, telling me what I couldn't have and what I could have – as long as it wasn't too awful. I was sick of them saying I shouldn't do this and that and dress up like I did: I never seemed to be able to do the thing they wanted right. I didn't like being bossed round and I'd had it all my life practically, and then I met Miss Dorothy Arbuthnot, whose brother Harry had been one of Dad's drivers, and she told me about her mother and how they had a nice extra bedroom. That's when I decided to leave home for good.

Mum and Dad were both much against me doing it, but they couldn't stop me, and Dad knew Harry, so the Arbuthnots weren't strangers in a way. I'd always had a money-box with the hole you put the pennies in, and I'd had a lot of money in my bank-book from when I'd left school, even. And I filled up two suitcases, but I had to leave my paintings behind.

I got ten shillings a week and my keep, and I was old Mrs Arbuthnot's companion in her big house at Wayville. She was a person from England who wasn't silly or sick, but she took little funny turns, and Miss Dorothy Arbuthnot didn't like leaving her mother alone while Harry was working in the motor trade, and she was away being the boss of a huge great grocery shop in town.

A woman came in to do the washing and heavy house-work but, really, I ran the whole place. I got old Mrs Arbuthnot's meals and she'd sit in her chair crocheting while I made conversation or sang to her; and I'd go to the shops, and to the market up in town every Friday night with a basket. And old Mrs Arbuthnot had some toffy dresses with lace from England that I'd alter for her to make more modern, and I'd do some ironing and she used to like all her tablecloths starched and folded a certain way (those old tarts from overseas were fussy-bags). And I'd get the tea for the four of us, and I'd done my cooking classes at St Joseph's, so I could roast a chook or do different stews, or nice tripe or grilled chops.

I missed my classes with Miss Madge, but the Italian man next door had a business of painting plaster statuettes, so I started going in weekends to help him. I'd rub the statuettes down with sandpaper and undercoat them all over with shellac. I had my glass jars of standard colours, and I painted the Whistling Boy and Miss Mischief and Cherry Ripe and the Bon Ami pals. Those statuettes were sold, very expensive, by the big shops in Rundle Street.

Mum wouldn't hardly communicate with me, but Dad came round a couple of times to see how I was getting on. Chooky was always there playing his violin and on Saturday nights we'd go off to the Soldiers' Club, where everybody particularly liked it when Chooky played the flute and I played the piano and sang about the sweet violets of early spring which came in whispers and thrilled us both; and Chooky would join in with

"Of love un-speak-a-ble that is to be,
Oh! promise me; Oh! pro-mise me."

Chooky said sex wasn't a sin, really – the Lord gave you man-and-woman sex as part of your body, and if you were inclined that way people oughtn't to condemn you for doing that sort of thing. And Chooky said there was no law in the world or in the kingdom above to say that sex wasn't real. It was a thing that was given by God for two people to go together, and that was how it was supposed to be done decent, even by the animals, to pair them.

I'd never had much of a fancy for sexual business; I

didn't know much about it. But you always tripped over something or other sometimes in your time – you found out things without wanting to. Though when they whispered about men's things I didn't know what they were talking about: how the man had the doings to do for the girl and the girl had the doings to take it. Taking it all round, it sounded very intricate and silly, and a lot of it would make you sick. Because a girl told me once how some men were that rude they wanted to poke their tongue in your mouth. No one ever tried it with me – that'd be the last thing I'd let them do: I'd bite it off.

I'd never been interfered with by anybody in my life; Chooky never touched me ever how I didn't want him to. He didn't push it: if I said No, that would be it. He never bossed me round, because he was scared I'd walk out the way I'd walked out on Arnold Bywaters.

But Chooky said it was just natural for people to be naturally sexified, and I started worrying how some natural-born ladies might even be like it, and it wasn't always sort of wilful if you went and did something wrong. It happened to some girls and if I ever let him, it might happen to me, and unmarried girls having babies got put in a place up there at Fullarton and had to work in the Fullarton Laundry. There was a double row of almond trees in front of that laundry, and in springtime the blossom was beautiful. They used to let the girls out to go down Unley Road altogether in a pack, and when their babies were born they were taken away from them.

Chooky and I started talking about getting married, but whatever we said it stayed a complicated mess all round; with Mum and Dad not wanting Chooky, and Mrs Hopps only wanting a Catholic, and Chooky wanting whatever I wanted, which was a proper church wedding dealt with by a legal religious minister, because my whole family over home were high class people, beyond what you ever thought of.

Then Chooky went to see this married woman friend of his from the Soldiers' Club, who was a member of a church in town that was a very favourite place for people who were a bit above the others for getting married. But if you weren't a real good person you couldn't get a wedding there, they wouldn't have you; you had to be perfectly religious and not have done anything wrong or they wouldn't take you in and praise you up, and say that you were a good person getting married.

So Chooky's friend had a conversation with the Church of England Minister of that church who she knew very well. She explained to him – he must believe it – that it was dramatically honest with no immoral business in it, but she had this girlfriend who wanted to get married (not because she had to personally – she wasn't in trouble), but her parents were against it, and did he think it would be proper for her to get married without their permission, because she was twenty-one, and would he kindly perform the marriage ceremony.

The minister said it was a bit unusual, but if the husband-to-be was a good man, and if the wife-to-be was quite clear that she religiously thought it would be a good thing, and as long as she had turned twenty-one, he was agreeable to do the job without parental consent. But it couldn't exactly be a church wedding, as a lot of the people in his audience mightn't approve; so if we came down to his home on South Terrace that very Friday night he'd do us privately.

Friday night was market night, so I went up there as usual in my ordinary clothes with my basket and got a few things, then met Chooky and his friend and her husband who were coming with us to be the witnesses. I left my shopping on the minister's verandah and we went inside, and he was waiting in his religious uniform with the Bible and everything ready, and he did the wedding ceremony and I married Chooky Hopps. We sang a hymn and had a little chin-up and the minister gave us a signed photo of himself. Chooky had forgotten to buy the wedding ring so his friend had lent me hers, and next day Chooky went and bought me my own personal one. But I didn't wear it, because Chooky and I had decided that it was just his business and mine that we'd got married.

After the wedding I went back to Mrs Arbuthnot's like I always did on Friday night. And I didn't tell Mum and Dad, or anybody else, that I was married.

A lot of the things growing now are changing the atmosphere. And a lot of the vegetables in the ground and the fruit that we used to have for years are all changing their mixture. A fruit we knew a certain way for years was usually nice, but you get one now and it's not like it used to be — you wouldn't eat it even, perhaps. Specially melons and things that have juice inside and hard skins. Because things are not growing like they used to. And there are grasshoppers destroying a lot of the ground where things are growing. And bigger things are coming up out of the ground, like those black things that creep; cockroaches, and things of that sort. You hardly ever saw them long ago, but now they're down low in the garden and they're coming up and eating all the roots of your good plants up top, and that kills the plants. The ground's gone so hot and dry underneath, they're coming up to get the dampness out of what we've got up top. So you don't know, do you.

I didn't go in the same bed as Chooky when I got married first; I kept being scared I might get one of the seeds when it was time for my own whatever it was, so it was quite a while before I could make up my mind to have anything like that.

Then Chooky got a motor-bike and sidecar, and took me for rides to different distant places where he'd spread out a rug. And one evening round Mount Lofty way, I must have had a silly fit on and Chooky got a mad trick of patting me, and I must have been a little bit not watchful and I never realised he was in where he was and it hurt. I must have thought what it might be like if it had happened, and it had.

One Saturday when we were riding down to Victor Harbour on Chooky's motor-bike, who should be coming on in the car beside us, but Arnold Bywaters – of all the people! He saw me personally in my pixie-hood, sitting in the sidecar, next to Chooky in his belted trench-coat and gorblimey cap; and then Chooky put the speed on and left Arnold Bywaters behind. A few days later I got a postcard, forwarded on from Honeychurch Avenue: "Seen you again after a long wait. But, as usual, too far out of reach."

Arnold Bywaters was still very rapt and went to see Mum, hoping he'd get me back. For a while after that he started coming to Mrs Arbuthnot's in the night and knocking on my window, and I was scared Mrs and Miss and Mr Arbuthnot would hear him.

Then I started losing my monthly things and feeling a bit sick in the mornings, so I went to a doctor and he said I must have been having some turns with my gentleman friend because I was nearly three months pregnant. I felt awful. And then I started showing I was pregnant, and I was one of the sort that wouldn't like anyone to think that I had to get married, so I went and told Mrs Arbuthnot that I *was* married.

Mrs Arbuthnot didn't think it nice for me to live in a house with her unmarried son, when I was a married woman. I couldn't go back to Mum and Dad because they wouldn't have Chooky in the house, and as I couldn't stay with the Arbuthnots I thought we ought to tell Chooky's mother.

And when we did – even though I wasn't a Catholic – she didn't take it too bad. She just said she'd move another bed into Chooky's room and I'd better come and live there, too, till we found a place of our own.

So Chooky had his white enamel bed with brass rails and a white honeycomb quilt on one side of the room, and I had mine, matching, on the other. But Chooky was his mother's pet, she sooked up to him, and couldn't get over him acting loving and bringing cups of tea to me in bed. Mrs Hopps said her Chooky wasn't cut out for that.

But I got on very well with Mr and Mrs Hopps. They liked company and I could help with the housework – when I got going I kept going for hours: if I wanted to get done, I got done.

I always cooked the dinner on Sundays, so Mrs Hopps could make sure Chooky was going to be looked after. She said he wasn't hard to manage; she'd brought him up on the plain food. He liked roast beef dinners and fish with parsley sauce and a nice rice custard with a cut up banana; and baked roly-poly and narcissus blancmange. She'd open her recipe book and say, "Now pick out a pudding," and I'd have to make it. The first steamed Mount Lofty pudding I made, I lifted the lid all the time and when I took it out it sank.

Mrs Hopps was a stickler for her little back kitchen being tidy, and every time any friends came she'd get Mr Hopps to paint it. Mr Hopps was always painting, because Mrs Hopps was the sort of English person who liked to have home parties. When there was a party, Chooky and I played our duets and Mr and Mrs Hopps would do the cakewalk and sing the old English songs. The piano woud be going and the floor bouncing, and one of Chooky's sisters was married to a chap who had a boxing kangaroo that usually performed, and people would get a bit drunk and have arguments out in the street.

I didn't believe in showing myself off strip-naked to anyone, even if he was my husband. So I never got undressed down to having nothing on in front of Chooky – even if I was just going to change my top clothes, he'd have to wait outside and read the paper or something.

Chooky never used to pull his clothes all off in front of me, either – he knew I didn't like it. And I'd have my bath and Chooky would have his bath, but we never went in the bath together or anything. Though sometimes Chooky might want me to scrub his back . . . but he'd have the curtains round the bath and the flannel over him, so I wouldn't see anything showing. When he was going to stand up and all the rest of it, I'd be out.

I'd never seen a man close up with nothing on, ever – I never really saw Chooky. I hadn't had a lot of wakeup to how men were, and how they went this way and that way; I wasn't interested in seeing who had a bit of what's this or whatever else (only when you were married to a man you couldn't help seeing a bit sometimes). If I'd ever been at the beach and a man came out of the water and just accidentally he had nothing on, I'd have had a fit and run for my life.

When you were going to have a baby, you couldn't do anything, only wait for it to come. I didn't worry about whether it'd be a boy or a girl – I knew I couldn't rub it out and draw it in again. I just waited to put up with what I got.

A friend of Chooky's had lent him his motor car in case I

had to go to the hospital in the middle of the night. But Chooky was a devil for playing billiards at the Soldiers' Club, and this certain Friday night he'd taken the car away to go to his blooming billiards, and I was in bed and it started coming on like wind in my stomach. I felt so awful I didn't know what to do, and Chooky still hadn't come home. I couldn't walk round much, my legs seemed stiff. I got on the chamber because I thought perhaps I wanted to do something – but nothing happened, because it was the pain of the baby business. I called out to Mrs Hopps and when she came she nearly had a fit. Then Mr Hopps came, too, and they lifted me back on the bed, and it was going on and on and on, and I felt terrible, and I couldn't do a thing.

Just as they were saying we'd have to get some help, Chooky came home. Mrs Hopps sent him over to the Unley Post Office where there was a telephone box, to ring up the hospital to warn them I was coming. But the silly goat was that nervous he couldn't find the hospital's number, so he came rushing home again in the car with the telephone book. Mr Hopps found the number in a minute, and told Chooky to get back for his life.

They put me in the car and as we were going down King William Street, the town clock struck three. When we got to the hospital I was in the hang of a pain, and frightened to get up on my feet even. Mrs Hopps, who'd come with us, kept walking close behind me with her skirt spread, so if the baby fell out she'd catch it.

But the baby stayed stuck and I went till half past two the next afternoon before I had it. They put my feet up high and my back down low, but they couldn't give it a push or anything. I was trying to be brave and sensible, but it was agony, like I was poisoned; I kept calling for Mum, and the youngest nurse was crying. They said it was about the worst hardest presentation they'd ever seen in all their time, and they were really sorry for me.

They had to use forceps and I think they forgot I wasn't cat's meat, as I was torn from earhole to breakfast time. When I woke up I was knocked out, and it felt like I was sewn up with barbed wire. I couldn't wee, and I had a tube up me, and on top of that I had a bunch of grapes as big as apples: between stitches, tube, and apples I didn't have much crutch left. I was frightened to cough, laugh, or do anything – I must have stretched myself to bits.

She was an extra big baby with a mass of red curls on her head, and nobody had red hair in the family. The first thing she did when they handed her to me was blow off in my hand.

Mum didn't want to come and visit me because she didn't like Chooky, and she'd never wanted me to marry him. But Dad made Mum come and he wanted her to take the baby and hold it, but she wouldn't touch it even – she didn't want to know a baby belonging to Chooky Hopps. So Dad went crook at Mum and took hold of the baby and put it in her arms, and when it started to cry I thought she'd drop it.

Before she was born I'd had a sort of idea that babies were very much like little animals, and that, provided they were warm and well fed, they spent most of their time asleep and didn't present any particular difficulties: I soon found out my mistake. My redhead was a saucy little girl, pretty lively, and she did a funny lot of things and had ways of her own – if it didn't suit her you couldn't get round it. I called her Lillian, after Lillian Gish who was in *Broken Blossoms* with Richard Barthelmess, and had hair like a cloud round her head and a pursed-up rosebud mouth and big eyes.

There have been big storms up north recently and there have been hailstones and things, and one time they had big sheets of ice coming down out of the sky and it was filling up all the rivers and flooding all the townships round about. It was a terrific thing. One of the worst things ever known. They reckoned it was Armageddon: it's like the whole world is turning over. Last night from four o'clock onwards it was shocking, and today they reckoned we were going to get hailstorms this afternoon, but it changed all of a sudden: about eight or nine o'clock this morning the earth moved round a bit and it got pretty warm. But the sea was coming up in great big flops, and it was very deep and dark. They got a lot of sharks last night, and those other smaller things that aren't sharks but they look a bit like them. They're the sort of fish that have small bones instead of great big ones, and they've got thick white flesh. Hundreds and thousands of them came in with the sea today, because it was flopping and smashing away so much. People were picking them up and cooking them on the beaches, and having parsley sauce and all with them.

One night Chooky came home to say he'd left the tobacco shop and was going back to be a butcher at his Uncle Jim's.

Chooky had always liked bones – he'd liked bones from when he was just a little bit of a lad. When the school holidays were on he'd be over at Uncle Jim's in Beauville playing butcher's shop down the back by the stables, chopping up bones with an old blunt chopper, keeping his fingers out of the way like Uncle Jim had shown him. Then he'd make out he had customers and start weighing the bones and putting them in bunches and wrapping them up.

Chooky had liked bones so much that when he left school, Uncle Jim took him on, and he worked in the butcher's shop till he went to the War. To start with, he didn't even chop bones — he mainly did deliveries and cleaning up. His first job in the trade was to dip the saveloys in a bucket of red dye and the frankfurters in a bucket of yellow.

When we moved to Beauville I used to push Lillie around the streets in her pram. She was a good-looking kid with great big violet eyes and dark red curly hair, and even when she was crying she had a very pretty voice. I pushed Lillie from our rented house in Fifteenth Street up to First Street, where Granma and Granpa Hoff had lived, and ladies in pinnies would look up from polishing their front verandahs, or watering their front gardens, to smile at us as we went past. Granpa Rodda had built every one of those houses, all exactly alike, so it seemed as if Beauville had personally belonged to him. I was his grand-daughter, named after two Queens, and, pushing Lillie, I liked to think of myself as the secret Queen of Beauville.

Granpa's house with the turret was still on the corner of Redruth Street, but now the two Dr Gesters lived in it — and Fatty and Skinny Gester had an organ in there, and a harp and a grand piano.

Sometimes I'd stop outside Priddle's bakery and look at the wedding cake in the window with its icing-sugar scallops and dots and doves; but if Priddle's boy stared at me through the glass I'd hurry on – he had a queer way of looking at you, as if he could see through your clothes. Or I'd push Lillie along the Port Road and stop off at Sticky Thomas's lolly shop to buy some of his special Beauville rock. We'd go past the Gasworks Hotel with its windows wreathed with coloured glass tulips and roses and lilies (Chooky often sneaked in there for a quick one when he was out delivering). And there was Doody's newspaper shop where Chooky placed his bets, because Mr Doody was the Beauville SP bookie. On top of the shoe shop next door was the billiard saloon where Chooky went to play night-times, if he wasn't down at the Beauville Soldiers' Club.

If it was summertime, the window of Uncle Jim's shop had a pig's head in the middle and parsley sprigs stuck everywhere round the trays of chops and the rows of roast beef and legs of lamb; and sausages were looped up artfully so they wouldn't drip on the meat and send it sour. Though I didn't think it was really a good idea to have things like that stuck right under your nose; I reckoned Uncle Jim should have kept his meat hidden away for buying in a closed-up clean chamber. When you saw all that stuff in the window it made you wonder when you got your meat home . . . you didn't feel like eating it, after you'd seen it lying about dead.

But in wintertime everything was different, because Uncle Jim was a Michelangelo in meat. He'd carve chilled blocks of fat into things of beauty and put them in his window on exhibition: motor cars of lard, a sailing ship of suet, the Queen of Angels Church with its spire and belfry and open doors all cleverly reproduced in dripping. When he fashioned a scene from the gold diggings in Victoria he had all the characters: prospectors, women, children, and even dogs. The chilled fat models were jointed and moved by strings, like a marionette show, and you couldn't get near the butcher's shop for sightseers.

If I saw Chooky in the shop I'd go in to say Hello. When

any old fidget came in, grizzling about her meat being tough, Uncle Jim would recite his favourite expression: "The Lord made the meat, the devil made the cook, and the angels made the butcher." He was a small man with the narrowest shoulders of anyone I'd ever seen. Because his shoulders were so little it looked as if his head was large, and his toupee jumped every time he used the chopper.

Chooky liked doing deliveries on the cart – he said it was where he got his good health from. His customers trusted him so much they'd leave their door keys for him if they had to go out, and he'd let himself in to put their orders in their ice-chest.

Chooky was always bringing home best-tasting rump steak and undercut that was as dear as anything. Chooky loved meat, even the fat – he said the fat kept his organs oiled up. But I didn't fancy eating so much blood meat, and after a while I only liked a bit of veal if I did it nicely with onions. People that ate and ate meat were like semi-animals, a lot of them. Some women that overate meat grew big chests and huge bottoms. Too much meat could give you the cramp, because it caused your blood to stiffen up instead of going through neatly; and it often affected your eyesight, or made your head get itchy.

Chooky started giving me left-overs from the shop at the end of each week: the cow hocks and pigs' trotters and sheeps' tongues, and any scraps of corned beef and whatever else was around. So every Saturday night, just to please him, I'd have to put them in the copper and boil them up to make brawn for his Sunday breakfast.

Chooky seldom took me out with him to places any more, and I missed playing our duets. Most night-times Chooky was either in the billiard saloon or over at the Soldiers' Club, or some other boozy place. And even though I'd had Lillie, I hadn't put on any weight and still had my golden hair and blue eyes. I wasn't one of those women who put so much face cream on, they fed the fat under the skin and grew hair on their face – I was never a hairy person. I had no extra hair growing on my body anywhere. Hair was ugly under your arms and if it got damp it was nasty, so I used to put some stuff on that killed the roots before they came up through.

Chooky took me for granted, he didn't seem to respect me; I had to take a back seat – everyone came before me. He expected me to stay at home and scrub his white butcher's coats and blue butcher's aprons, and iron his shirts and starch his collars for the Soldiers' Club. Before we were married, Chooky couldn't do enough for me because he thought I might leave him like I'd left Arnold Bywaters, but now it was another story. Sometimes I wished I'd married Arnold Bywaters and had a wedding veil and a silver horse-shoe and a shower bouquet of Christmas lilies and delphiniums. Or maybe if I hadn't started any matrimonial affairs with anybody, and had kept on living with Mum and Dad, I would have had one of the new French bois-de-rose frocks with hat en suite, and even a Mongolian fox fur. Chooky hardly gave me any money, I was expected to economise with everything. And then one day when I said I needed some huckaback for a new apron, he said he'd spent all he had at the Soldiers' Club and if I wanted any I'd better go out and earn it.

Chooky didn't think I'd take him seriously. He thought he could rule me, but I couldn't take much more of that. So I spoke to the lady next door, who said she wouldn't mind looking after Lillie for a few hours every day if I found myself a job. I reckoned with my high-bred background over home, and my brain being more active than most people's, I could do almost anything. I was used to superior types of people, because Mum wouldn't speak to just anybody if they weren't decent socialites. Being a high standing lady herself, Mum had often boasted that she was friends with Dame Nellie Melba and other tourified mighties who wintered on the Riviera to dodge snow-storms. And I always looked nice and everyone thought I was fairly well-to-do and I thought people who went to high class tearooms would prefer to have someone like themselves serving them.

I started looking in the newspapers, and one day I saw an advertisement for a waitress to do morning teas and luncheons at the Argonaut Tearooms up in town on North Terrace. I'd been there a few times with Mum, and knew it was the place where all the socialites went. The advertisement said the waitress should be experienced, but with my background I knew all about everything. And they wanted a waitress who was single, because if you were a waitress you had to flirt a bit with the men customers to keep them coming back. So I took off my wedding ring and went up to the Argonaut and interviewed the manageress and, because I was me, she pretty soon offered me the job.

Then I was Miss Alexandra May Rodda again, in an orange dress with a white collar and a little black bow in the front, a white apron and a white cap with black velvet round it. There were orange place-mats for the morning teas and white tablecloths for the luncheons, and I arranged the vases of gum-tips and Iceland poppies. Sir Tom and Lady Wavertree, Mrs Ivor Peel, Miss Girlie O'Brien, the Misses Dymphna and Trixie Pride, the Bonythons, the Barr-Smiths, and all the other top Adelaide social people came down the stairs from North Terrace and I smiled at them like they were an equal and they treated me back decent, with respect. The well-known doctors who had their brass plates out along the Terrace had their own particular tables in the smoke-room, and one long table of doctors who didn't smoke got together down the front in the ladies' room. After they'd finished their fricassees of this or that, or their something on toast, they'd play dominoes.

My favourite doctor was young Dr Loach, who was a merry type, and one lunchtime when I hung his coat up in the ladies' room, no one was about, and I got inside it and folded the sleeves round me. But there were sliding windows between the ladies' room and the smoke-room, and when I looked up Dr Loach was looking through, laughing his head off.

The doctors didn't like anyone hovering round when they were talking about their cases, but one day I heard Dr de Mole telling the others how he'd just operated on a human ostrich and removed from her stomach ninety-three tacks, fifteen pennies, three collar-studs, and a miscellaneous assortment of nails, screws and safety-pins. He said she'd been disappointed in love and had tried to assuage her pangs of unrequited affection by making her stomach a veritable dustbin.

With my first pay I bought a pair of Champagne shade pure silk stockings and a tin of Fleur d'Amour talcum powder. I liked listening to the other waitresses talking about their glory boxes and evening frocks; and how one of them got water-on-the-knee from overdoing the Charleston at the Bullfrog Club. I often wondered what I'd do if young Dr Loach asked me to go to a dance . . . I imagined myself in sunset-pink chiffon: a sweet pea or a wild rose dress, with a big many-petalled unnatural flower on my shoulder – something unknown to horticulturalists, a cross between a peony and a giant carnation.

But I always had to go home to Chooky, and if you went and got married you had to put up with a bit of sexy business sometimes. Men were all due to what their breeding was, and people reckoned some couldn't help it if they had to be playing round and touching and tickling. Though we weren't a terribly at-it-all-the-time couple. Chooky had to have permission, he couldn't just do it when he wanted it. Any lady who wasn't absolutely rooky didn't want to be bothered with it too often – it wasn't really a thing you went mad over, especially when they'd been smoking or using grubby old butcher's tools. If you had a kid already, and didn't want to get any more, you had to be careful.

There were lots of ways of being so, but it was a pretty tricky affair. The lady next door said some wives got so worried they even soaked a bottle cork in petrol, or mixed up methylated spirits with butter, and stuck it up inside themselves; or you could take some female pills that shut you up tight so your husband couldn't get in.

Dr Skinny Gester said he wouldn't give me any of those pills, but gave me a rubber cap (as approved by Dr Marie Stopes, with large solid rim) to stop the pregnancy seeds getting through. I didn't fancy fiddling round inside myself with that queer rubber cup, so sometimes Chooky would wear a sausage-skin thing. But sometimes he didn't, and then I found I was expecting again.

I had to leave the Argonaut Tearooms long before I was bulging out in front, because those doctors had X-ray eyes and would have objected to being served by a person in my certain condition.

There've been moons that have turned upside down, and gone off bang and all; though I forget what they call it when a moon does that. And the moons have been queer lately – they've been huge. The night before last there was the biggest moon anyone'd seen for two hundred years. It was a great big round thing that might have been made of new brass. It was shiny, with no marks on it – no bubbles or nothing. And so bright, like a big sun. It lit up the whole sky. It was terrific. I thought it was the sunshine going down it was so bright. Sometimes when you see the moon or the sun up in the sky, you can't believe your eyes at the bigness and the way it's going.

The Kewpie Maternity Home, round the corner from the Beauville School, was run by Sister Grace Brecknock, an old girl very qualified, who'd been one of Queen Alexandra's nurses in England. You could book in with Sister Grace if you were having a baby, and she'd telephone your doctor or she could see you through your time herself, so you didn't have to bother with all the expensive hospital carry-on.

One day I felt a bit funny so I went down to the Kewpie, and Sister Grace looked me over and said I'd better stay there: she didn't think the baby was far away. But when she rang for Dr Skinny Gester, he was up in the Hills, playing golf with the son of Sir Somebody, the very old royal man Dad used to drive round, who'd had the mansion up at Mount Lofty. Dr Skinny was so long coming down from the Hills, that by the time he got to the Kewpie, Sister Grace had delivered the baby and tidied it up and put it in a cot. Dr Skinny she she'd done him out of a job.

It was a baby boy, so properly big built he looked as if he'd get up and walk. He had golden hair like me, but he was the image of the baby picture Mrs Hopps had of Chooky sitting up in his pram. I named him Ramon, after Ramon Novarro. As he grew older his hair got a sort of reddy look, so Chooky called him Chutney, and pretty soon everyone called him Chutney, even me.

I had to go to the hospital up in town weeks before the next baby was due, to have special massage and looking after. It was a worse agony trying to have her than when I'd had Lillie — it went on so long; but she went funny altogether, and then she died. She was a nice baby who'd gone the full nine months, and it took me a long time to get over it, though Chooky didn't seem to take it too hard. When they'd been a soldier for years, things had to be really dreadful before they got upset.

After that I had a bit of a false go once or twice: the pregnancies didn't last very long before I lost them.

It was a hard thing to bring up a child right from birth — anything could happen that'd knock you flat. I didn't want to be made pregnant again because of the little girl who died and my couple of slips. And, in any case, it had started to be the Depression, and I didn't see any sense in having kids you couldn't afford.

And the lady next door and other people, too, had told me they thought Chooky was going with somebody else and having the time of his life. Once I even asked him and he made a terrible scene, so then I thought the best thing I could do was shut up. But I didn't want him interfering with me if he had another tart outside — I was fussy about my penny ha'penny place. Even an apparently nice decent man could go with someone and catch something that he didn't know he had, and he could give it to his wife straight away.

Chooky wasn't too bad as a rule for lying all over the bed, but I started not liking sleeping anywhere near him. I couldn't be bothered with cuddles, I hated that huggy-muggy business when he kissed me on the lips, even if it was a very special occasion. I'd often sleep down the other end of the bed, so Chooky's feet would be next to my pillow. Then I decided to make up the bed in two halves, with two lots of top sheets and blankets, and pillows down the middle. It was a difficult thing being persons and all. I was married to him, but I couldn't put up with the blooming sex business. If a husband was respectable he wouldn't tread on a wife and make her feel like it was all he wanted.

As the Depression got worse, it was a battle for Uncle Jim to keep the butcher's shop going, though he still helped the Beauville Mission with odds and ends for the children's free dinners. Uncle Jim had to put Chooky on short time, but Chooky used to feel sorry for the women with big families who were struggling, and slipped in bits of steak when they asked for soup bones.

When Uncle Jim was forced to put Chooky off altogether, we had to sell the silver teapot Lillie had won in the Bonny Baby competition and the Mount Etna family brooch and my other bits of jewellery. Even if you were on rations, you couldn't make them last the week, so Chooky went in for pie-eating contests at dance halls to get a good meal. He paid four shillings and got his money back if he could eat at least twelve pies; but the first time he was sick before he could eat that many, and had to forfeit three-and-ninepence. He hoped to get himself up to polishing off twenty-four pies to win the prize of a pound, but he never did.

Chooky tramped everywhere trying to get any old job, but there were so many others out of work he didn't have much chance. He got so sick of tramping round he swallowed his pride and went up to town with his violin to try and earn something that way, playing on the footpath outside the big shops in Rundle Street. There were unemployed banjoists, flautists, mouth organists, steel guitar players and other violinists all along the street; unemployed nightingales sang popular songs; Piccolo Pete was up on the Beehive Corner, and once a man spat on the footpath and poor old Pete thought it was a shilling. Chooky had a trick of romantic eye-rolling for the ladies as he played "The Pagan Love Song", and some days he came home with a few shillings, but other days he hardly made anything.

Times were so bad, Dad'd had to sell some of his hire cars, but he was able to help us out with the rent. Mum unstiffened herself enough to send over some clothes for Lillie and Chutney. Though the kids always had shoes for school, they had to stand up for free books.

Chooky went grape-picking up the country; then he had an idea he could make wooden toys and sell them to the shops. He'd seen a Mickey Mouse on a stick with wheels you pushed along, and when you pressed something Mickey did a somersault. Chooky reckoned he could use his butcher's saw to make Mickey Mouse toys out of old packing cases; but he spent a week trying to make one and then gave up.

The newspapers kept writing about the poverty in Beauville, and called us Beauville people dilapidated individuals; the newspaper cameraman took pictures of people queuing outside the Mission soup kitchen. Socialites started coming down in their motor cars – some even had chauffeurs – and giving out eiderdowns and babies' clothes and iced cakes and all sorts. One paper had a picture of Lady Wavertree handing out oyster patties in Beauville; and she called it her Mission of Mercy.

Though some rich people lost their money and jumped off tall buildings, it seemed most rich people didn't feel the Depression much at all. They were still there on the social pages of the newspapers in their gold and diamond jewellery, leaving for overseas (to pass down the Nile at sunset); or strumming their banjos and ukeleles (bathed in sunshine at Victor Harbour); or watching Phar Lap romp home in the Adelaide Cup (wearing their ensembles of grotto green, that was the new season's colour).

A road climbed up from Beauville to the golf-links and the parklands and the flash houses where the socialites lived. Now and then I'd go up there with Lillie and Chutney and have a walk round. Some of those mansions had been there since Hector was a pup, and there were wistaria arbours and statues and fountains. And inside them were high-class fashion people . . . and I could iron anything – I'd watched Mrs Quigley all those years. It was a tricky business, but I was not that careful it wouldn't matter if it had cost hundreds of pounds from dressmakers. I thought perhaps Dad could give me an introduction, because he must have driven lots of those socialites about.

Dad wrote me letters to three ladies, and the third one I called on said she had a friend who wanted an ironer. So I went to see Mrs Paris Bertram of Brougham Place, and she got out a couple of dresses for me to iron, to see if I was as good as she'd been told. Those dresses had been made by Miss Goldsmith of North Adelaide, who dressed the elite, and they were so perfectly made you could have worn them inside out.

Mrs Paris Bertram took me on, and she was so pleased with my professional ironing abilities that she talked about me to her friends, and soon I was a visitor to do ironing at two other stately homes, for people who were well-to-do millionaires nearly.

I never scorched anything for anyone, or dropped the iron, or made a mess. And I ironed Mr Lance Buzzacott's good tailor-made suits and his evening shirts with the complicated stiff bit in the front that fastened with pearl buttons, and sometimes there was a waistcoat thing, too; and I stretched them out nicely and never squashed the collars up, or left a single little fold in them. And Mrs Lance Buzzacott had dresses with skirts that were pleated right down with a silk lining inside, the same shade as the dress, and it was a hard thing to do but I taught myself. And Miss Bubbles Greenwood who drove the canary-yellow sports model Ford with blue bumper bars and red leather trimmings, had lace nighties you could have gone to a wedding in; and I ironed her crepe satin petticoats and brassieres and pants. And old Mrs Greenwood had lace-up corsets made of linen, intricate, with double seams, that pushed her out in front, and I ironed them as well.

Often the things would still be on the line drying when I

arrived, or brought in anyhow, all flopped in a basket, and I'd have to separate them. There was a way to do everything, and I ironed embroidery upside down, gently on a pad, just a little bit; and some things were made of such special material, if you used a hot iron you could melt them.

I got paid well for ironing, and the ladies used to often give me something very nice. Sometimes they'd wear a dress to a ball or a big wedding and they'd only wear it the once, like socialites did, and then they'd give it to me the day after. I got a ton of clothes that were really too flash for me to wear – I didn't exactly look poor, but chiffon with sequins would have looked peculiar in Beauville.

Thousands of years ago people used to go up in the sky from the mountains and get up near the moon and walk on the stars somehow. Mum's family came from the Bavarian Mountains (that's where all the snow goes up high) and lately, where those mountains are, the moon was so big and hot (which is only once in every hundreds of years it happens), those stars in the sky were melting and bringing that snow-water down on us all here. And that moon was even hot enough to melt all the cold stuff in the sky where the snow usually used to be. So I don't know, I'm sure.

Mum had always had a nice figure with beautiful legs, but she started getting thinner and thinner; she went down and down. Though her long golden-brown hair didn't have any grey in it, the doctor said it was taking all the strength out of her body, and if she didn't have it trimmed to a normal size length she'd lose her life. So Mum went up to Rundle Street and got her hair cut short into curls, and the hairdresser plaited two cut-off pieces and pinned them on like ear-phones round her ears.

Some people said it was unlucky to keep cut-off hair, and Mum's health didn't improve. Then the silly old ass of a doctor said it must be on account of her teeth making her gums bleed, and she was passing the blood through her body, and she'd sort of dried up. So Mum went to the dentist to have all her natural teeth out, and false ones put in.

One day when Mum came back from shopping, the berries like little plums from the trees in Honeychurch Avenue were everywhere over the footpath, and she tried to step over them but she slipped. Mum hurt her leg that bad Dad had a Chinese doctor come to see it, because they were pretty good with that sort of thing. And the Chinese doctor investigated Mum's health as well as her leg, and said she was suffering with pernicious anaemia. They gave Mum blood transfusions and all, but they couldn't seem to cure it; and then she went right off her feet and a nurse came to look after her. But Mum was a bit fussy and didn't like a stranger giving her sponge baths or being too familiar. So the days I wasn't ironing, I'd rush over home on my bike and get Dad off to work, and then wash Mum and rub her and take her to the lavatory and help the nurse make her meals. When Dad came home from driving of a night I'd have his tea ready for him, and then I'd dash home to Chooky and the kids.

One morning when I was with her, Mum wasn't too good at all. She couldn't talk or hear me or anything – her mind was gone, and her feet went stiff. While the nurse was telephoning for the doctor, Mum just threw her head back and was gone.

It wasn't as if Mum and I had ever got on well together as a mother and daughter, except only occasionally; I didn't miss her that much. But one day after she died, I was walking down the street and I started running to catch up to a woman in front of me. I thought it was Mum, but of course it wasn't – it was just the colour of the cardigan she had on. Mum had always been partial to that shade of mauvey-blue.

After Mum died, Dad retired from driving and got Mrs O'Harris, a widow who lived opposite in Honeychurch Avenue, to come and keep house for him. Mum had hated Mrs O'Harris and, when there'd been a Mr O'Harris, O'Harrises used to have awful rows. One time Mr O'Harris made Mrs O'Harris pack up her things in a case, and he put her out the door and said, "Don't come back," and threw the case after her, and it hit her on the head and nearly knocked her over, and she was holding the baby.

That old tart, Mrs O'Harris, had always been after Dad, and she pushed her way in and – I didn't know what the hell he did it for, or how she got him to do it – Dad ended up marrying her. And she was a rotten thing, bad-tempered, who looked like a barmaid out of the pub. She wasn't a nice lady. Nobody liked her in the street, even. Mum wouldn't have wiped her feet on Mrs O'Harris. You couldn't compare her with what Mum was (you wouldn't put your best sheet with a piece of dirty rag you washed the floor with).

Then Dad had a sudden stroke and it left him a bit peculiar in the head, and he had to stop driving altogether. His royal blue car just stood in the garage. And then it disappeared and I thought it was funny, so I went into town to the place where you registered the cars. There was a girl in charge of the office where they kept all the data about who, what, and which; and, though she wasn't supposed to – but because all the other attendants had gone out to lunch – she let me look up Dad's car in a big book. And I found that bloody old tart he'd married had changed the car into her name, and given it to her son. I was sure Dad wouldn't have signed that car over to her, so she must have done that somehow off of one of Dad's signatures or something. Dad wouldn't have given her a wheelbarrow, let alone a car.

And Mum'd had a lot of very valuable jewellery, and one day when I went over to Honeychurch Avenue, I looked everywhere but it had gone: the old bitch must have pinched it: she'd taken the whole bloody lot and I never got anything.

One of Granpa Rodda's houses in Redruth Street was up for sale for a song. It had white stone round the windows, and a verandah with lacework, and seven decent size rooms with jarrah floors and pink and black marble round the fireplaces. The front fence was one of those that had the wood all polished, and there was a gate in the middle where you walked from the footpath straight to the front door. And either side of the front door were special little red glass windows that shone up like the house was on fire, nearly; and up on a brass plate was the name of the house: Linga-Longa.

The Depression was easing off and Chooky was back working with Uncle Jim; and I had what I'd saved from ironing, and – though that old bitch of a tart tried to stop him – Dad had given me a good certain amount for looking after Mum. So altogether we had enough to buy Linga-Longa; and, when we did, the old tart nearly had a fit when Dad said I could have the piano from Berlin and the big brass vase hundreds of years old with dragons wound round it, and the snake gods for handles, and the man with four arms from Indian literature on top of the lid. And I took all the paintings I'd done that were still in my old room, and the Sleeping Beauty doll Granma Hoff had given me, and the framed photograph of me as a kid in my dotted Swiss pinny, and the one of me wearing the Mount Etna family brooch.

The man we bought Linga-Longa from had spent most of his time away travelling, and he'd planted up the front garden with things from Fiji Island and other tropical overseas places. There were hardly any plants in Australia like them — it was amazing to see them grow in Beauville out of their own original atmosphere. Some were historical and only flowered a certain time every so many years; some were treacherous and bit you with their leaves — they stuck in you sharp like a dagger; some started off from a bulb on their bottom to grow into a bush with flowers on its stem like a lot of little white bells. That bell plant was real Oriental, and its flowers came exactly on Christmas-day and the main go of Easter. They were something to do with the orientals' religion, and when the moon shone they lit up all white and transparent, and you'd swear they had electric light bulbs inside them. They hung down like glass bells on a Christmas tree and it was really remarkable. Everyone in Redruth Street stopped to look at my bell bushes.

Next to my lucky jade plant was my deadly poison tree with its white angels' trumpets that dangled, and anything that ate any bit of that tree would double up in a minute. And I had a bird-of-paradise plant, and a queer striped daisy that came out in millions and had its seeds in sausage sort of holders.

Round the back, past the big gum tree that had been there hundreds of years, from the Aborigines' time, was a fruit garden, with a passion-fruit vine over the lavatory; and an apricot tree, an orange tree, a lemon tree that had lemons with no spots, and two fig trees with itchy leaves by the water tank. One had figs with a pale green skin and bright pink insides that tasted like peaches. The other tree had figs with a creamy colour skin and insides just like strawberry jam, as sweet as anything, and Lillie and Chutney couldn't stop eating them. There were tons of grape-vines all along the side fence by the shed: the great big winey-purply ones that were Chooky's favourites, and the white ones with no seeds.

Down the very back was a tree with old-fashioned foreign fruits, smooth skinned, that were a golden colour. They took a while to get ripe, but when they did you could tear their skin down with your fingers, and they were soft as jelly inside with a vanillafied taste that was so scenty it made you sneeze. Those fruits were real Island things, Japanese or something, and they came in hundreds. But when the wind blew hard they'd fall in the grass and burst. And then the blooming pigeons all came down from everywhere, and the red and green parrots, and those other birds that made a noise like a whistle.

But I often put out crusts of bread for the birds; and I could get any bird to come to me, even one I met fresh for the first time. And magpies didn't peck me, cockatoos would sit on my finger and yabber-yabber away.

I wasn't scared of anything. If a savage dog looked as if it was going to eat me, I'd say, "Hello, old boy," and next thing I'd be tickling its nose. I could contact anything or anybody, really – whether they were old or looked fierce, or what.

One of our new next door neighbours was an amateur veterinary surgeon who'd learnt it all himself, and had worked in with circuses and taught horses to jump, and reckoned he'd brought the first bulldog to South Australia. I used to help him a lot and one time I was under a horse's neck, holding its head down for him to pull its tooth out with an awkward instrument. Another time, when I helped him stitch up a dog with safety-pins, he tied one of my stockings round its muzzle so it wouldn't bite us.

A lot of times, it's hard to explain, you have funny feelings about things. The sort of thing that's in the back of the Bible – weird like that, where people used to have special ways they buried bodies and they didn't decay or go away as usual, but one of these days they reckon they'll come up. Because a lot of times they bury people for ages, and when they have, for some reason, to look down into where they've been buried, they haven't even gone funny. There are a lot of queer things we don't know about. Especially if you go overseas where the pyramids are.

Though Lillie and Chutney were both quite different personalities, there wasn't much trouble with them, whatever. Chooky was extra serious and a bit bossified at making kids try and behave themselves and do things right: Lillie and Chutney had to do what they were told, or they'd get whatoh.

Chutney kept on coming up from boyhood, the image of his father; and he was a gentlemanly little bloke, pretty shrewd and quiet. He had two poached eggs every morning, and gave me all his paper-round money, except for what he spent on a tin of condensed milk every Saturday night (he'd poke two holes in the top and drink it straight down). The sea being in the family from way back, when Granpa Rodda came out on the *Buffalo*, Chutney had an ambition to be a sailor, so his birthday parties always had a nautical theme. I'd ice a logcake, ends trimmed to shape, in white and stick on a cardboard sail to make a smart yacht with Life Saver sweets for portholes and lifebuoys and red candles along the deck. I'd make other boats out of quartered orange skins full of jelly, with wafer biscuit sails, and small iced sponge cakes with funnels of cooked macaroni. They'd sail on a sea of chopped green jelly in my big meat dishes, along with starfish biscuits cut out with my star-shaped cutter.

Lillie learnt tap-dancing from a high professor fellow in town, and did her tapping practice at home on a little wooden mat in front of the mirror. She was naturally double-jointed and could tap-dance bent over backwards, till her red head was touching behind her backside; and she could tap-dance on the tips of her toes. Lillie wanted to tap-dance in the musical follies they had at the Tivoli, but Chooky said he didn't fancy the idea of his daughter going on the stage and throwing up her legs and being nearly naked and all. So when Lillie came to leave school, she ended up by being apprenticed to Mr Polkinghorne, a tailor up in town.

First Lillie got put on to the table, sewing buttons on and doing buttonholes; then she started sewing up miles and miles of trousers on a machine. Polkinghorne's girls didn't get any tea breaks, and they weren't allowed to talk – if you spoke by mistake, Mr Polkinghorne would sing out, "Stop your gabbing." If he was in a funny mood, and a girl had her back towards him, he had a habit of rolling left-overs of material up in a ball, and taking aim: and when it hit her, she daren't laugh. Every Friday afternoon he'd switch the power off early, and each girl had to take her machine to bits and clean it out and oil it, and have it all nice and ready for Monday; and Mr Polkinghorne came round and inspected everything, and then they were allowed to go home.

Lillie always walked quick, and any girl that walked quick got sent on messages. So Lillie took boxes of suits to the railway station, where they'd have to be weighed on the weighbridge. Lillie was a good-looking girl with her red very curly hair and violet eyes, and the boys would be giving her wolf whistles, and she'd be that embarrassed.

At Christmas time Mr Polkinghorne used to come out and ask, "Any of you girls got young brothers?" and then he'd sell grey melange off cheap. Lillie bought some for Chutney, and I made him his first suit with long trousers.

And when Lillie bought some fawny-coloured worsted for a costume, she made the skirt and I made the coat; and Lillie wouldn't wear that costume till she'd saved up for new shoes, new underclothing, a new hat and a camellia nosegay for her lapel.

One day Lillie was sent with a parcel to a place in Chesser Street that had the funniest old lift. She got up to the second floor and delivered the suit all right, but when she was in the lift again and pressed the button, it started going up instead of down. Lillie panicked and got bamboozled and pressed all the other buttons, and then the lift got jammed. She was trapped inside for hours, till some workmen rescued her. When she eventually arrived back at Polkinghorne's, old Polkinghorne didn't believe what she said about the lift and gave her the sack.

Then Lillie went to work in a drycleaning shop. But one day a girl came in with an evening frock she'd had wrapped up for a week. It was a beautiful pink lace, and she'd been sick on it, and the stink was something dreadful. The counter was packed with customers but everybody went for their life, and the girl had the cheek to stand there and laugh. Lillie had a very weak stomach and ran out the back and vomited her head up.

Then Lillie went to work in a brush factory, and learnt the trade of making not just brushes for sweeping the floors, but the very fine brushes with carved handles the hairdressers did their hair with. It was a most complicated business, and Lillie stayed there for years and ended up being the head one in the factory.

All my ironing mob – Mrs Paris Bertram, the Buzzacotts, the Greenwoods – were the high Adelaide families, from England and all, with beautiful homes and lovely dresses.

They were so kind to me they couldn't have been better, and their socialite friends who were also people of that nature liked me too, because, Mum's family coming from the Bavarian Mountains, I'd been brought up more or less in the social way. I had a proper feeling for things that were nice; I hadn't been allowed to say wrong words, or go round with my dress half hanging off, or fiddle with people's possessions that didn't concern me. Though I wasn't one for blowing out my flag, I had some sort of a look about me that caused the topmost top people to trust me (if they even wanted to confide something that was a bit behind the curtain, they'd tell me straight, where they wouldn't go and tell someone else).

When Mrs Paris Bertram left to live in Melbourne, and the Buzzacotts went overseas, any of their socialite friends would have engaged me for ironing. But Mrs Justin Julian – whose husband had Julian's, the big drapery shop up in town – was looking for somebody that wasn't just anybody to be a general lady-help to her full-time. So I went along to see Mrs Julian and she was good-looking, with her hair done lovely and a house full of the latest modern appliances and a well-mannered little boy. And as I was getting a bit sick of Miss Bubbles Greenwood and old Mrs Greenwood, and thought I'd like a change from just ironing, I said I'd be agreeable to have Mrs Julian engage me.

But it turned out the Julians were a bit beyond what I'd thought they'd be. Mr Julian was wild, with an eye for the women, and Mrs Julian was jealous. One time she found a lipstick in his pocket and hit him and they had a hell of a row and she never spoke to him for weeks and wouldn't sleep in the same room or anything. Yet Mrs Julian kept nicking off out herself, and having some of the highest businessmen in town taking turns to come and call for afternoon tea. I'd let them in the front door, and she'd be on the sofa in only a little silky bathrobe that was ready to fall off and leave her in the alto: I'd try to sneak on my toes so they wouldn't hear me listening, and they'd be talking and laughing and carrying on. And Jasper Julian was a difficult child, always up to mischief, who'd destroy things like other children wouldn't think of; and he'd go to the cupboards and pull everything out, and you wouldn't be surprised if he set the house alight. And the things that kid used to say! – one time when Mrs Julian was entertaining a gentleman friend, Jasper walked in and told her to stop showing off her pussy (and she gave him such a smack over the head she nearly knocked him out).

She wasn't a lady at all, but just an ordinary threepenny bit sort of person, though she thought she owned the world. She was as rough in her speech as the kid was, and she was a snatchy crabby thing who treated me as if I was a dog. It wasn't the sort of refined society I was accustomed to, so I gave Mrs Justin Julian my notice.

After that I was lucky, because I was invited to work for Mrs Norbert Packard, whose husband had the select furniture manufacturing business. Mrs Packard was beyond reproach as a decent woman. She trusted me with her valuable jewellery; she knew I wouldn't pinch anything, not even one teaspoon. I kept her house nice and tidy, I ran the whole show, and Mrs Packard wouldn't let anybody boss me with two words.

If Mrs Packard was doing any dressmaking, I'd have a look and pass my opinion as to whether I thought it was too big or too small or what. And I did Packards' ironing, and made them apple pies with good pastry if they were having a party. And if they had a great big banquet I'd cook the chooks and turkeys all stuffed, and the little savoury things you passed in first, and Mrs Packard always referred the table settings to me. I had a sort of mania for doing things like that. I was used to it from days gone by with Mum: I knew about fish knives and cool drink glasses and all the other certain things that came in handy if you had to go into a millionaire's house and work.

When it was Miss Sylvia Packard's wedding, I decorated the wedding table; and I ironed her water-lily cream heavy satin wedding dress and the silk and delicate things that went under it, and the things she took away for her honeymoon – I did the whole lot, right from the hankies to the last bit. I was invited to the wedding and the wedding breakfast, too; and there were four or five bridesmaids, and toffy men in evening suits and stiff collars; and I had a lace frock and a straw hat with roses on it, and my hair was still like gold, and some people nearly thought I was the bride.

And then when Miss Sylvia Packard-that-was had her babies, she'd bring them to visit and if Packards went out of a night, I'd stay on in the nursery. Sometimes there'd be some of their friends' babies there, too, and I could have as many as eleven children to be minding. All the cots would be round the walls, and I'd have to change the babies, and feed the ones with bottles, or turn the ones that woke up. Even if the Packards and their friends stayed out till three o'clock in the morning, I still waited, and then Mr Packard would take me home to Linga-Longa in his limousine car.

Mrs Packard treated me like her other daughter, almost; and the time she fell off a jetty and hurt her legs a lot, and the bottom of her body, and was very ill, I was like a nurse with her. I looked after her for ages as she couldn't get up out of bed, she was helpless. I'd give her a bath and a shampoo and rub her all over and change her pants for her and everything.

The sun's different to what it used to be. It's so bright you can't hardly look at it, or it'll burn your eyes out nearly. It lights up the house like it's on fire, or as if someone's left all the electricity on. When the sun's that way inclined, it's absolutely red-hot; and the heat's taking the moisture out of the stones and the stuff they're using to make the big new buildings, and before long they'll be all falling down. And the stars in the sky are different to what we've ever known them, and we've got aerial things shooting through the sky that we haven't seen before, and sooner or later it's going to go off bang, once, and the whole lot's going to collapse . . . Takes a bit of believing, doesn't it?

Meat was rationed in the War, and the amount of ration tickets Uncle Jim got every week didn't keep him supplied with anywhere near enough meat for the amount of customers he had. So Uncle Jim had a chap that went round a lot of slaughter-houses up the country, buying spare tickets (you weren't supposed to, and some got caught doing it). It cost some money, but it meant the butcher's shop kept its customers.

Chutney left school to work in the shop, but his heart wasn't really in it. When he was out delivering he'd be always stopping the cart to collect any thrown-out odds and ends for the War Effort, and he kept asking customers if they'd save their newspapers for him. Every scrap helped towards Victory, and our back yard was full of old tyres and goodness knows what, and Chutney got a medal for nearly topping the state in collecting.

Chutney kept on being a real Rodda – they were all sea-mad, all that push. When he'd been a kid, Chooky had made him a little tin boat, and Chutney used to sit in it down the yard and pretend to row his boat along in the sea. It seemed to just be in Chutney to be like that, and as he grew older he could row a real boat nicely, and he was good at jumping off jetties and swimming, and he went in the sailor boys' club that taught kids to learn how to look after themselves and fight, in case we had anyone come invading the place.

Chutney was pretty well ahead in knowing how to put sails right or engines or implements or anything; and when he was exactly old enough, he joined the proper Navy. Though he wasn't tall, he was fairly weighty and had good-shaped legs for when he wore his white sailor's shorts. And he liked to have neat socks pulled up tight underneath him, and he had very nice feet when he had his sailor's shoes on. Chutney was about the smallest and youngest and tidiest sailor that was in the War, going over to the Islands on a great big warship. Though, taking it all round, he was more than just a sailor – he was a real naval man.

Some of the Island women were very good looking, so in the Navy it was part of the regime to give out the things like sausage skins to our boys. If they went ashore they always had those things to put over themselves, because they didn't want to get any disease or get the women into trouble. Providing Chutney with those things was a waste, because he wasn't one to go with girls a lot.

It was malaria country up in the Islands; it was a different place there altogether. Every place had its own look about it, and in the Islands they had big rats and crocodiles, and what was even in the sea could be terrible.

Sometimes, sailing from Australia, the warships used to run out of drinking water and, if they saw an island that looked neglected, our boys would sneak ashore, a few at a time. But some of those damned Japanese might be hiding in the top of the palm trees, lying on their bellies with their guns; though, if you looked up, you couldn't see them. And as soon as our boys put their foot on the ground those Japanese up in the trees would shoot them down. Some of Chutney's best pals were killed, and our other boys couldn't go ashore and pick them up as they would have got shot as well.

The Japanese used to be always shooting somebody you didn't want to lose. While Chooky was round the Soldiers' Club being patriotic, and Lillie was out dancing, and Mr Hopps (who'd come to live with us after Mrs Hopps died) was asleep in his bed, I'd be sitting up thinking all the time, feeling scared that Chutney might get hurt. Till I pulled myself together and made up my mind it was no good knocking myself rotten and worrying about what I couldn't help, and making myself sicker than what Chutney would be if my worry happened, and then it'd be worse than ever. You couldn't do anything, so you might as well shut up and forget.

And then the War ended, and when our boys came home from the Navy, other boys were all on tiptoe, waiting to see if they had any spare sausage skin things to give out.

Chutney got back to Linga-Longa for Christmas, but he was only home on leave for a month. He was one of the better naval men — one of the most proficient and worthy — and had to return to the Islands to clear up after the Japanese had left. He was very brown and thin, and looked as well as possible, with a row of medals on his chest and strips on his sleeve telling you what he was; and he had a new automatic watch which he never had to wind up.

We all went over to Honeychurch Avenue on Christmas Eve and had some of the pedigreed champagne Dad was keeping for Lillie's wedding, though the old tart didn't give us much of a welcome. We had six at Linga-Longa for Christmas dinner, as I asked the funny kid in from across the road (his mother had to work in the Railways Christmas-day, and only left him a bit of fritz). The ice-chest leaked and the ham went bad, but it didn't seem to matter: we had port wine and lemonade with our turkey, and Lillie got the giggles, and Chutney filled up the bath and put her in. Lillie couldn't get up for laughing, and was sopping wet and had to strip and get dressed again; and then Chooky got out his violin and I played the piano and we did some of our favourite duets.

Chutney brought home a carton of Chesterfield cigarettes and heaps of tobacco for Chooky, and some singlets and pyjamas for Granpa Hopps, and a whole lot of white towels and pillow-cases for me, and some tropical sheets made of silky muslin stuff for Lillie that would do to make curtains or hankies or even blouses. And he brought a cord-velvet dressing-gown, wine shade, for his Granpa Rodd, but Chooky grabbed it.

Lillie tap-danced at the Soldiers' Club all through the Wartime, and went to the big dances up in town looking dressed like the Queen. We used to make her dance dresses together and they were beautiful things, all satin and lace and net and low necks, with shiny beads and sequins sewn on everywhere. Lillie liked her dance dresses to be a violet colour to shade in with her eyes, and she had a lot of jewellery with purple stones. She wore expensive brassieres and scanties she got cheap from the wholesale people, who reckoned when she had them on she'd look so nice she'd be a good advertisement for them.

I was an expert dancer and Mum had been a champion and Lillie took from us. She had certificates and silver cups and medals for her ballroom dancing. She could do the difficult dances with scissor steps and half-moon steps and double-time twinkles; and the even more intricate dances, that were usually only done over in foreign places, like Buenos Aires and Rio, where you got swung off the floor and twisted and tipped up, till you were just about floating before you came down again.

Lillie wasn't the sort of redhead who freckled fifty spots to the square inch – if she did get a freckle she'd mix up lemon juice with something and bleach it away. She didn't have any scorched or burnt places on herself because she carried a sunshade in summer, so her delicate skin wasn't spoilt by the sun; she washed her face and neck with warm milk before she went to bed. She was a well-built girl with dimples in her flesh, and a firm-shaped bust that didn't wobble, and a tidy backside, and nice calves on her legs that ended in neat feet that fitted number three shoes. She always had a green dress in her wardrobe because it brought her good luck. She wasn't a mucky sort, just wearing a thing anyhow; if a dress wasn't perfectly right, how Lillie thought it should be, she wouldn't have it.

Lillie could have had a hundred boyfriends if she'd wanted them, but she wasn't fussy on boys – she never went round showing all the material she was made of, or got in and out of cars showing nearly everything she had. She didn't care for someone praising her up to try and make out they'd get a bit on the side if they were getting anywhere. You couldn't trust some people for five minutes. If I didn't think any of Lillie's dancing partners were suitable to fit in with her way of going, I wouldn't have them in the house. And Chooky was most particular about who went out with his girl, and would tell the wrong type where to go in a certain language you wouldn't like to hear.

Lillie had a boyfriend who was a food crank and said eggs hardened the arteries, but he liked lambs' tongues in piquant sauce for breakfast. Lillie had a boyfriend who was the wobbling type – he wobbled from side to side when he walked into the sitting-room; he hung his head and started wobbling worse if anyone spoke to him. Lillie had a boyfriend who was a Yank in a tailored uniform, and he even gave her all the things you couldn't get: nylon stockings and scented soap and cigarettes for Chooky; and they ate American hot chocolate fudge pie and drank Singapore slings. Then the funny kid from across the road came over to introduce his cousin, Eric Riddle, who'd just come back from the War.

Eric Riddle was a gentleman most of the time who thought he was somebody and liked himself a lot and did his shoes nice and his nails and all. He was toffy-looking with a tall standing-up soldier's figure and a little black moustache: he was a particular type of man the women fell for, and straight away Lillie was in love.

Eric went back to being a men's-wear salesman in his civvies and, every night they weren't out dancing or at the pictures, he'd be round at Linga-Longa, cuddling Lillie in her good-luck green dress, and Lillie was a changed girl. Her mouth looked half an inch wider from Eric's kisses; she was all the time blushing a pretty rosy red, and I suspected she was thinking secret sexified thoughts.

Early this morning it looked like the whole sky was on fire. It's the stars coming down out of the top and setting light to the snow on the mountains – and that snow's melting and flooding out all the countries overseas. This is a different kind of thing to what we've ever had for hundreds of years. The whole world's turning over – it's like Armageddon. All the heated stars up top are sailing through the sky, and it looked as if it was alight and flying in fire. And it was going up and round the moon; and then some big mountain-top slipped in the Alps somewhere or other, and came down and flooded everybody out. The world's gone the wrong way round and it's moving all the time. There's something queer going on in the atmosphere that we don't know of, and they reckon pretty soon there'll be earthquakes and landslides and I don't know what. And there are these ants that came years ago out of the ground, deep down in the earth – and they eat blood, and they've been coming up lately with what's going on underneath them. They've got some strange poison in them, and if they bite you they give you that funny thing people get in their lungs. They try to bite you because of your blood. And it's all happening in places where they've never ever heard of it before.

Lillie had a handkerchief luncheon and a kitchen evening and a something-blue party and married Eric Riddle and went to live in Sydney; and Chutney was still in the Islands, and it seemed the family was all moved about to get in some other atmosphere, and I started having the horrors. Nothing went right and I couldn't hardly sleep, and those nights when it was a waste of time going to bed, I'd get up and mend the socks or go for a walk round the garden. Everything looked different, with the plants not seeming to be mine and the poison tree trumpets dangling queerer than ever and the striped daisies all shut and not like daisies any more. And I'd look up and watch the moon in the sky – and the stars would be shifting about and shooting round, real big ones; and I'd think of Lillie in her wedding dress with a raised-up flower pattern in the satin and a mile of train. And then I'd think about Lillie when she was a kid and how, if she didn't want to do something, she wouldn't . . . she was a tough little thing who'd give the boys a belt in the earhole – my Lillie had to be the boss.

But she'd married him, smiling all over her face, and gone to live somewhere else. It would've been funny, after she'd gone away sort of for good, if I hadn't missed her.

When I was over at Mrs Packard's I kept stopping work to examine my looks in the mirror. I felt just like a hollow doll with the stuffing knocked out of me, though I'd put on a good weight and had a nice flushed face and my skin was still so smooth as silk I nearly wasn't able to feel it even. But some of my gold hair was silvery, and my violetty eyes had changed colour to a darker blue, and my eyebrows had gone a different shape.

I felt better when Lillie wrote that matrimonial bedtime carry-on stank. I wrote back that I'd been holding my nose for twenty-six years. But I told Lillie not to let it turn her against him – the damn fools didn't seem to be able to help it, and Eric didn't appear to be unreasonable. He had a lot of better things about him to be considered.

I never knew what was going to happen next, that bad time.

One day Chooky came home from the butcher's shop with a pink and white cocky one of his customers didn't want. We called it Queen Adelaide and she used to sit up on my pagoda and talk like one thing, and as soon as she saw Mr Hopps she'd say, "You old bugger," though we didn't teach her to say it; and Queen Adelaide couldn't bear you to pick up a hammer: Chooky was hammering something down on the verandah, and she grabbed his thumb and he lost his thumbnail through her. We used to get Queen Adelaide in her cage in the corner by the pantry at night and cover her over, and she'd still be talking away underneath. But it started getting so I couldn't stand Queen Adelaide talking, so Chooky took her back to the shop and gave her away again.

And right after that, Mr Hopps went over to his daughter's place and asked for a glass of water and fell back in his chair and died.

Then Dad started getting a lot more peculiar in the head, and then he just sort of went and died as suddenly as Mr Hopps. And I don't know how it happened, because it was meant to come to me after Dad died, but the will had been played around with so much that the old bitch of a tart got the house and the property and the contents and everything of what had been Mum and Dad's and my home in Honeychurch Avenue, North Unley. And she sold it all, and went over to Melbourne to live with her son, and I never heard of her again.

Then one of the young aeroplane pilots had to fly back from the Islands with a very special message to the Governor of South Australia, and Chutney got permission and hopped on, too, and I'd kept his room all nice and tidy and ready for him. And, apart from Chutney suddenly arriving home for his visit, that night was a strange one that gave you a feeling there was something about. It almost wasn't a surprise when Chooky and I woke up to hear a rumbling and people yelling; and then everything started to fall down and shake, and the people were yelling worse and going out in the street. But Chutney came and stood at our bedroom door and said not to mind, it was only an earth tremor – Chutney knew what was happening, because they had them regularly overseas in the Islands. That night of the earthquake was when the cracks came in the corners of the rooms of Linga-Longa, and they stayed there ever after.

Chooky bought a secondhand silvery-grey Austin motor car that was like a little hooded vehicle, though if you didn't want the hood you could shut it down like a baby's pram. Chooky liked travelling because of being in the Army so long, and after he got his car we started having a hectic time travelling round a lot.

One Christmas we took our camp-beds and went over to Sydney to see Lillie and Eric. Chooky took his oilstone with him, so he could sharpen up all Lillie's knives.

Lillie was a bit of a fuss-pot over her crystal and occasional tables and velvet pile passage carpet; Eric was one that liked to have a tidy house, too. There was a sun-room and an inside lavatory and a cosmetic counter in the bathroom, and kookaburras laughed in the garden. Lillie had red roses and purple irises and three lemons on her lemon tree, and she said she wouldn't be able to even buy herself a pocket hanky for many moons because of paying off their house. But she looked on the bright side of things, though Eric was flat out being the head of a new big men's-wear department and often wasn't home at night till all hours, and he was that nervy he could've taken up smoking. When Eric got home he ate like a horse and had three pieces of cake and five pieces of toast and honey, and when it came up for tea he'd have roast beef and six potatoes and peas and carrots and bread-and-butter pudding and a pint of milk, and finish off with dry biscuits and cheese – he'd eat so much he'd nearly burst his belt. And we had barbequed sausages and went to Bondi Beach and Chooky had an incident where a centipede bit his toe, and Eric got full and abused us.

Lillie had a black cat, and there was everything in the Sydney shops you could lay your tongue to, but Lillie couldn't afford to buy anything and said she could come back to dear old Adelaide tomorrow.

Then Chooky sold the Austin and bought a secondhand utility motor car, and we took a tent and our camp-beds and drove right over the Nullarbor Plain to Perth. There was only one thin road like a dirt track through the desert, and it was thousands of miles away across there, and it was usually a place where there were no farms, there was nothing: if you got lost you'd stay lost.

And it was a time in Australia when the Queen and the Duke came away out from England, and they got to Perth just when we did, and they lived on board their royal ship, the *Gothic*, and we went down to the edge of the scene at the wharf to see what they looked like.

Chooky and I had accommodation in a hotel with a top-storey balcony to look from, and there was a big turn-out one night at Government House. We saw the Queen in a most wonderful satin dress as she drove right past underneath us in one of those low carriages Dad used to drive, and she had a diamond crown on. She seemed older than she was, like a more ladylike person; the Duke was a Greek man; and they had the real king and queen way about them (of course, I was named after two queens – I was born the day Queen Mary, who was the Duchess then, came; only her proper name was never Mary – she was Princess May of Teck).

But that time in Western Australia there was a polio scare, and the Queen and the Duke took special precautions. Everyone had to keep six feet away from the royal visitors, because that was the approved quarantine space. And all the Queen's and the Duke's food was washed in antiseptic: they lost a lot of weight in Western Australia.

The moon is made of ice rocks and things – it's not ordinary at all. It goes round different parts of the time and it changes. A few nights back I went out and looked about and it was the strangest moon I've ever seen. It looked like it had all little things flying out of it, and it was scarlet like it was on fire. And I've seen some big suns lately in the sky – big red suns, and even at different times of the day: early in the morning or late at night. The things up in the sky come in a different way than they used to. They've changed their look. And sometimes the moon leaves off a big shower of tiny little things flying off, as if little spots are breaking off the stars or the moon and coming down to earth.

Beauville started getting overrun with a lot of strange people who weren't like the other ordinary people. They were foreign, and their ways of doing things were different to ours. Ordinary people were polite to you and asked how you were going and were you all right, but some of these new people didn't speak to you, even if you spoke to them, and lots of them spoke their own foreign language in front of you.

The newspapers said how some New Australians smoked sex-drug cigarettes, and read publications prohibited by the Vice Squad, and wore suede shoes, and carried brief-cases, and cooked dishes foreign to the true Australian menu like goulash and sweet-and-sour and pork en casserole, and were just as likely to bang you or stick something in you if you slept on your front lawn in summer.

The Italian girl from across the road who was getting married invited me over to view her trousseau. She said it was the Italian custom to have seven of everything, so, hanging from the picture-rail along the walls, she had seven new dresses and coats and petticoats and dressing-gowns . . . I'd never seen anything like it in my life. And all round the room were tables spread with seven pairs of brassieres, pants, shoes, gloves; and seven hats; and seven of everything else you could think of. I went home and told Chooky I couldn't believe it, even though I'd seen it.

Further up the street, our side, lived a brother and sister who were always arguing out in their back yard in Dutch; till one day she yelled in English how he'd tried to throttle her. She had to make him peach wine that was very buzzy, and he kept it under his bed and drank a bottle every night. One day she sent him into town to get a lemon tree, and he purposely came home with a grapefruit tree because she hated grapefruits.

When the two Doctor Gesters put their house, that had been Granpa's, up for sale, it was bought by a husband and wife from some queer place overseas. Their name was so foreign nobody could say it. They were aristocratically flash with proper good manners, and everybody called them the Count and Countess.

The Count was a big fat-faced bloke who wore a monocle on a black cord and a carnation buttonhole in the lapel of his impeccable suit; the Countess was a small frizzy-haired lady with a refined atmosphere. They reckoned they were friends of overseas nobility and royalty and turned Granpa's house into a School of Social Grace where they taught poise and posture, the art of walking and relaxing, table manners and ballroom courtesy, easy conversation and social charm. Socialites who wanted to circulate with comfort and dignity came down the hill to Beauville to learn vowels and manners and the etiquette of the vice-regal curtsy, and how to be more polished and poised and elegant.

Seeing I was who I was, I got the job of washing and ironing the Count's shirts. He wore fancy ones with lacy patterns and I'd wash them in Lux flakes by hand, and just squeeze them, not rub them all up. The Count's shirts were made with a special kind of ingredient in them, so I had to be very careful ironing or they might spoil.

The Count and Countess had a houseman from away over in the same very foreign place they'd come from, who'd been knocked about in the wartime — he'd had a very rough bash-up when it was the War over there. So he wasn't a beauty in a way: he was tall and thin, and looked just like a big thing you got out of a wax museum; and his face was a kind of a creamy colour, his eyes looked like they were made of glass and you could see through them, and he was twisted to billyoh. Even his toes and feet were hurt in different ways: all his life he'd had war troubles or accidents. But he was a hard worker and a very good character who didn't smoke or drink or swear or anything. And he was so clean with himself that he had a bath every day – and twice a day if he'd been working; and he rinsed his underclothes daily, too, as well as his socks and hankies, and then put them out to dry in the wind. And he never went round with his pants not done up, because the Count and Countess wouldn't have put up with that.

The houseman's name was as foreign as the Count and Countess's: it sounded like Joss House, so everybody used to call him that. Joss House came in when the apricots on my tree were ripe, and he and Chooky picked every one of them – they cut them all up and I lit the copper and we made a copperful of jam.

Then the amateur veterinary surgeon sold his house, and we got a new next door neighbour who hung strapless-backless Lolo bras on the clothesline, and peek-a-boo pants all frills. She was tall as a man with her hair set in dyed yellow angel curls, and she had false eyelashes and that much lipstick and rouge, and leopard-skin coats and red velvet dresses; and she kept boasting how she'd just about won the Miss Australia beauty quest.

Beauville people called her Miss Australia, but she was horrible and no damn good; you wouldn't have liked to introduce her to anyone polite. She was so bold and filthy-mouthed the way she talked – she said dirty things like a man might say if he was shickered or sexified: the sort of thing a man working on the road might say if he dropped something on his foot and let fly. She was vulgar and not nice at all. The time Chooky couldn't hardly believe how she fitted into her tight satin trousers, she came running after him up the footpath and stuck her backside out, nearly under his nose, and said, "There you are – have a good look."

She had a peculiar ginger cat that sat in her plants, even when they were sopping, and a normal cat wouldn't sit on something damp. She kept pulling all this blooming bluebell creeper off her fence and letting it fall in my place, and it wasn't growing in Linga-Longa's garden but hers. She smoked like a chimney and she drank like the devil – there were always about two dozen empty beer bottles on her verandah. She was usually in bed in a private way in the daylight; but if a man – the postman, the baker, or whatever – came to the gate, she'd run out almost strip-naked to speak to him. All the time, any day, she'd practically show her body off as if she'd just come out of the bath.

She had boyfriends all over the place, she went with anyone; she kept having different funny-looking men come visiting: she wasn't a good girl, she was a you-know-what going around getting paid for this and that. She had parties where we'd hear the male guests peeing out by her orange tree and telling dirty jokes. It got so I even had to keep my eye on Chooky, because there were a lot of times when if a woman saw her next door neighbour had a suitable husband, it mightn't be long before her and him got pretty friendly (though I didn't go as far as to think Chooky was going to get over the fence or anything).

I went out fairly late one night a few weeks back and the sky looked like it was on fire – it was red, and even when the sun was going down about tea-time the sky was scarlet. Not a soul in the place was supposed to smoke that day: anyone seen smoking a cigarette got fined, and it was the only time the whole world had been cut off from cigarettes – they banned them altogether. And the moon's getting so big and so hot now that it's melting all the block ice on the mountains, and that's why we're all getting flooded out in the rain. The whole world's out of pattern of proper light and shade.

The whole turn-out of time was funny. It seemed to go and come and twist around, and you never knew whether you were coming or going – half the time you thought you were going to meet yourself coming back, and you hadn't even been.

Once I'd sat on the Bible in my spotted muslin pinafore, playing Aunty Rose's piano that was draped with a black shawl embroidered with tiger-lilies . . . Aunty Rose had been dead as a doornail for years, and her shawl was wrapped around the Sleeping Beauty doll Granma Hoff gave me for passing my first music exam. That doll was in a box on top of the wardrobe, and she was still perfect with her real china face and golden curls and silk and velvet clothes – except that the elastic that held her joints together had perished.

Aunty Albertina's famous painting, "A Yard of Cats", was hanging up in the passage, and it would have been valuable in a museum, but Aunty Albertina left it to me in her will. My own paintings I'd done with Miss Madge were everywhere in Linga-Longa, but I didn't want to do any more because you got so many and didn't know what to do with them all. Over the hat-stand was one of Granma Hoff's plaster reindeer heads – but one of its antlers had broken off, and I'd never got round to sticking it back on. Further along the passage was the photograph of Chooky and the other blokes in his battalion before they went to the War.

Mum and Dad were there, young, inside the family album with the puffed-off leather cover, that had roses and cornflowers and chrysanthemums painted round its photo holes.

The older you got, the time or the atmosphere that made up your life seemed stranger – it was queer, you couldn't bet on a real nice plain coming-and-going sort of day at all. Time was always passing quicker in a way: you had that many different small things in between the big things, and you had to fit them all in together to get through the lot. And, with some of the small bits of time, you might think you'd have something done nice for a certain day, but, when you came to do it, time was either too slow or too fast. You might, for instance, be out travelling and you'd gone a long way, and you thought it was about time and tried to go home, but perhaps you were still going somewhere else.

Chutney had to leave the Navy because he'd started sleepwalking and it might be dangerous on his ship, so he came home and opened up a boat shop down the beach. He was a bit of a toff in a way, with a house up on the cliffs where he could see all the boats sailing. And he was a clever businessman with a saleslady that was good and self-contained herself, and she had enough brains to treat Chutney as a gentleman, and it all worked out and he married her.

Time was that mad, it seemed like Father Christmas made the world in the beginning. One minute I was a kid, sewing the hems of my sanitary napkins; the next, my monthlies had stopped quite suddenly, apparently, and I couldn't hardly believe it. And I'd thought it was all right, but damn it all, that day Chutney got married I had a cream lace dress on, and I was hurrying to get ready, and I was pulling my silk pants on, and I don't know what made me look but I saw this red mark on the back of them, and they were new to go to the wedding, and I got such a shock, I thought Hell, I won't be able to sit down in the church.

For ages I was always worried if I was going anywhere nice and dressing-up, so I'd put a pad on myself, just in case; and I got some pants with a little waterproof thing in the bottom. But after that time at Chutney's wedding it stopped altogether, and that was the finish of it.

After Uncle Jim retired, Chooky had managed the butcher's shop for him and worked it up to four bodies of beef, and about sixty sheep and lambs, and a couple of pigs, and two or three calves a week – though it didn't seem anything as good as the shop in the old days, with Uncle Jim's winter window-dressings and the sawdust on the floor and the blocks of ice instead of the electric freezer. When Uncle Jim died, the shop got sold and Chooky was getting on himself and said how he didn't want to be the richest man in the cemetery, so he just went relieving at a shop on the Anzac Highway. But Chooky couldn't get used to the electric saw and handling horse-meat, that was supposed to be as tender as anything and a bit sweeter than beef.

When Chooky gave up being a butcher altogether, he said how he missed the people and the company most. But he was always out somewhere with his mates from the Soldiers' Club and sometimes I hardly saw him. He'd go out fishing all night, even, and bring me home great big crabs and different fish. He belonged to the Beauville Cricket Club and he helped do the massaging for the Beauville Football Club, and he was still a bit of a devil and gambled a lot on cards, and he was a very good billiard player. There was a man in England who was just about the champion of the world at one time with the billiards, and he came out to Adelaide, and Chooky and eleven others played against him. The champion wiped off the other eleven, and my old boy was the last one left that he hadn't beaten: and he couldn't beat Chooky. The prize was the most beautiful billiard cue I'd ever seen in my life, in a special polished wood case with a lid you could lock, and Chooky won it. He wouldn't even let me touch it, but when there was a big billiard night at the Soldiers' Club he'd take it with him.

You had a nasty lot of little bits here and there in married life, but my later times with Chooky were best of all. He knew I wouldn't put up with hugging or lip-kissing, or anything worse that I'd never hoped for. Though we often thought something quite dissimilar of two certain subjects, we didn't fight or argue the point, we just went our own way (he wouldn't have been game to hit me — I'd have picked him up and thrown him over the back fence). Miss Australia was up to her tricks next door, but I'd never had anybody tell me since our early married times that I ought to watch Chooky because he was going on with any other woman.

Chooky arranged for Joss House to fix my back kitchen up and put a saucepan cupboard in, and he had an inside lavatory built and a new bathroom and a pantry. He bought me every kind of mechanical appliance stuff, like the big fridge, and the gas stove, and the washing-machine, and the television set when televisions came in. The frog was the emblem of some special day round Easter-time (it was some Eastern historical sort of thing), and every Frog's Day for years Chooky had got me one for a charm; so I had a family of lucky china frogs, different sizes, all along the mantelpiece.

When Chooky started getting dizzy fits and headaches and a nasty pain in his chest, the doctor told him he had to give up smoking as his lungs were grabbing. But Chooky's biggest trouble was that the doctor put him on a diet and he wasn't allowed to eat the fat on his meat. Roast beef had always been Chooky's favourite, but he gave it up because he wouldn't eat it lean without a selvedge of fat.

The Soldiers' Club had a special billiards tournament, and a lot of blokes came to play from the other states, and Chooky was round there with his prize cue day and night.

Once when he got home he wasn't very well; it was like he had a delayed war-shock thing that some people get, and he got a bit funny, and the doctor told him to stay home and rest.

A couple of nights later, Chooky was in our double bed, and I was sitting at the dressing-table brushing my hair, and I could see him in the mirror. He had the lamp on at the back of the bed, and he had his glasses on reading the paper – and then it seemed he was a long time just looking and he hadn't moved for ages. I thought it was strange and called out was he all right; I went round the bed to him and patted him but he never answered me: he was dead. I got such a shock. He'd died lying back on his pillow, reading the paper, so I was left just like that without a minute's notice.

Chooky had a very flash soldier's funeral because of being an Anzac, and they cremated him, and then he was put in his cavity in the big stone wall for the soldiers in the Beauville Cemetery.

I moved all my things into Chutney's old room across the passage, and I never slept in our double bed ever again (and it was lambswool on the mattress to keep you warm). I missed Chooky terribly – he'd been my pal for years. Chutney took away all his old things, but I made him leave Chooky's razor strop and the old sportscoat and green felt hat that had always hung over it behind the bathroom door.

But it was like everybody's mind had two ways: the earthly part and the weird part. And when my head was thinking the weird way, what got burnt and went into the wall was nothing to do with Chooky. Then it seemed that when your last breath went, you breathed your body out of your mouth and it turned into your spirit and it went up to the sky, and it was beyond the real knowing for us to exactly know what was going to be and where everyone was or wasn't.

Chooky had bought me a purple colour lounge suite like velvet. A lot of times when he'd been gone quite a while, I'd be sitting of a night in my chair and then I'd look round, and see Chooky sitting in his chair alongside of me. It was that plain I'd get a real jump. Of course it was ridiculous, but there was Chooky sitting in his chair like he always used to, with his cigarette in his hand. But he wasn't meant to be there. It was the weirdest feeling when you saw that sort of thing, and I wouldn't let any visitor ever sit in Chooky's chair.

There are subterranean storms under the mountains now, and the whole world's turning over again. All that was hot before is coming down and being cold and vice versa. We don't know what's going to happen in years to come, because a lot of the sea round the edge is going under, and things that live in the sea can't live there and are coming in on the ground and eating up all our fruit and vegetables. And a lot of big pipes are bursting because of all the waters coming in from outside, and crops and things are getting drowned. And we've been having big windstorms we've never known before, and even the stars are coming in occasionally. And a lot of times we have a big rain when the wind blows everything down, and all the prettiest plants in your garden get spoilt. No, we don't know what's coming. You can't stop it, so there's no good worrying about what you can't stop.

Lillie wrote how Sydney was a dump, though Eric had bought them a beautiful big home in a select area with a panoramic view; and it had wall-to-wall carpets and venetian blinds and a patio.

Lillie knew a lady who imported clothes from France – velvet and quilted satins – and she'd sell a model to Lillie for half price; and Lillie had nighties and bras with lace on them. My girl still had her firm-shaped bust and nice legs and curls in her red hair, and she brushed her long eyelashes with something to turn them up.

Lillie loved her garden but Eric reckoned she was saturated with pollen, and if he got near her his hay fever started off. Once he got away from the flowers and Lillie he was all right.

Eric was always attending conferences and conventions. Whenever he came home he was as bright as a tick, and Lillie wondered why, till she found a letter in his pocket and knew he'd been going off with another woman.

Lillie went to see a lawyer about getting a divorce, and then came back to live with me. She had the old room I'd shared with Chooky. She used to always get up early and have a wash and all the rest. She was a very careful one for looking after herself, for washing up and doing her fingers: she was a fuss-bag.

She was like my only sister, more than my daughter.

After I was done at Mrs Packard's, and Lillie had finished serving in the dress shop where she'd got a job, we'd come home and take turns to cook the tea. We worked in the garden together, and Lillie planted the gladioli like pink velvet and the snowball tree and the red creeping roses; and you could smell my garden coming up the street. We did dressmaking together, and in my sewing-room I had a perfect model from the waist up of Lillie's body. It was on a stand and you could make it taller or lower, and it had Lillie's bust and shoulders and the tops of her arms, and it was filled with some nice material inside you could stick pins in.

Lillie and I went to the pictures in Hindley Street once and saw a film on the secrets of sensible sex, with separate sessions for men and boys, and women and girls. It was so popular it was booked out and out and out: it was a good while before you could even get in. When we did get in, Lillie sat up the front and I sat down the back because they couldn't give us two seats together.

Lillie was often escorted out in the evening by Brigadier Wimpell, who was a widower, ninety-odd, with five sons and a Rolls-Royce car, though he usually rode a push-bike; and he had a children's playground named after him that had little bark houses where the mothers could sit and have their tea, and he wrote Christmas cards to people all over the world.

A foreign man who boarded round the corner was very fascinated by Lillie. He had his own washing-machine and was tidy and a wonderful gardener, but he always had a bottle of wine in his bag. He kept wanting me to rent him my back room, and he said he'd do my gardening, but I didn't like the thought of him living with Lillie and me and going in the lavatory.

Miss Australia hung nylon bikini pants in jellybean colours out on the line now. She was a sexy nasty type who'd steal the eyes out of your head while you were looking and swear she never had them. She was always wanting a lend of my stiff carpet broom, and I didn't like lending her anything. She had the cheek to want to borrow Lillie's clothes. I told Lillie not to let her: you'd probably never get them back, and if you did they'd stink of cigarette smoke or beer, and you might get a skin complaint.

I told Lillie I wouldn't let Miss Australia in the house – she might bring in a couple of her blokes for a lend. But Lillie was soft-hearted and used to go in next door and rub Miss Australia's back for an hour and a half when her monthlies didn't come. Miss Australia still went with who she wanted to go with, and lots of times things could go wrong. Once Lillie even waited outside in the car while Miss Australia went to see this pet doctor she had up in the Hills – and it never dawned on Lillie till afterwards what he might have been doing.

Some silly fool said why didn't Lillie try having a cigarette now and again for her nerves, and gave her some special ones from overseas that had a perfume in them. When Lillie smoked one she lost her breath and collapsed. She never ever got over it. I reckoned the stuff, whatever it was, in those cigarettes drained all the blood out of her body so she didn't have hardly any bloodstream. She seemed to be melting away. The doctor kept treating her for nervous anaemia, but that old doctor was treating her wrong.

Lillie got that bad I didn't know what to do, till Mrs Packard gave me a letter to a big bloke in town you had a job to get near. He hardly looked at Lillie before he said, "Good God, this girl's got gall-stones. She ought to be in the hospital."

So I got Lillie into the hospital opposite the park and they removed eleven gall-stones and she brought them home in a glass bottle to show me. They were huge, like those chocolate balls the kids used to buy. Two or three people we knew asked could they have one of Lillie's gall-stones to show what just could happen to you.

But Lillie stayed nervy and didn't sleep very well, so I'd let her stay in bed as long as she could.

One morning I got up first like I always did, and I had Lillie's breakfast ready and thought she was even longer than usual coming, so I crept up the passage to have a look. She was lying across the bed with the padded satin quilt in her hand: she had hold of it by one corner to toss it and she'd gone with it across the bed, and she was lying there with her eyes wide open: but my girl wasn't there, she'd gone.

Lillie was over by the jungle of pepper trees with old-time pincushion flowers and bridal creeper, in a garden of red roses – she'd loved red roses. There was a place left alongside of her, so I put a ticket on it, and it's still there waiting for me, and no one else can have it. So when I go I'll get put in my own place next to Lillie, though I won't be here to see.

Chooky hadn't sat in his chair all the time of Lillie's return, but now she was gone he started occasionally coming back again.

Then one night I saw Lillie, sitting as plain as anything – just sitting there like she used to on the sofa, dressed like she was when she was alive, and just watching. I wasn't scared, and after that, even if she didn't come for months, I had the feeling always that Lillie was near me.

It was something for people that were in good spirits with their own ones that had gone. You don't just go away and burn up or get buried – your spirit's still here; wherever the people you care about are, you are. There's a kind of vague area around us that we know nothing of: a kind of thing that we don't really understand in the air. It's another world sort of mystery, and there's no real dying – nobody really leaves the world. The world was a world before we knew it, even; even before Adam and Eve were here and all. And the real God is someone past the Son of God, and something that was here before we knew what we know: a spirit in the air that we don't really see, but we've got some kind of feeling – though if you're going to worry about it, it'll drive you crazy perhaps. But if you're happy about it, and you think it's all right that they want to see you, people like Chooky and Lillie often come to say good night when you're going to bed.

The world is changing now because all the stars in the sky are coming down, and the moon and other things up there are getting hot and making the earth hot, and when people get hot-blooded their nature goes up and they're doing a lot of things they wouldn't have thought of doing years ago. And those things they're doing turn into lung trouble and that's why there's so much diphtheria about, though some people are getting it from eating too much meat. The kids are getting it, too, at school even. It's going round the world like mad, you can't stop it, and pretty soon everyone will have it.

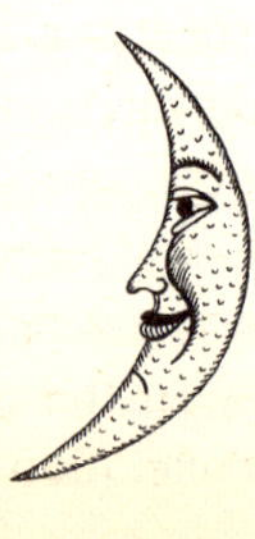

I'd worked for Mrs Norbert Packard for years, but I had to stop because I had a nasty fall coming home down the hill on my bike, and the doctor said I was working over pressure.

Mrs Packard was sorry to have me leave her. She wrote me a personal letter of condolence, and gave me a goodbye present of a unique antique object from overseas that must have been worth hundreds.

It was a statue of a naked lady made of marble, bending over a crystal glass bowl where you were meant to put goldfish, and the lady was supposed to be watching them swim round, and she held a modest little marble scarf thing in front of her while she looked. Only I didn't want to be fiddle-arsing about with goldfish, filling the bowl with water all the time, so I put in a ton of plastic flowers: tiger-lilies, hydrangeas, roses, larkspurs, carnations (and you could take them out and hang them on the line and hose them and they came up like new).

Mrs Packard's goldfish lady stood on a pedestal in the sitting-room with some of my other favourite objects: the purple lounge suite with its six cushion-covers embroidered in Bible pictures; the clock like the Town Hall clock; the Indian brass vase wound round with dragons; the Berlin piano; the Miss Mischief statuette; the collection of pinned-down butterflies, all originally alive; the silver serviette ring presented to me at St Joseph's by the Pope of Rome; the sideboard with my doilies in it —and on top was a hand-carved genuine oriental incense vase, old as the hills, that you put the stuff in, and scenty smoke came out; a photograph of me and Arnold Bywaters sailing on the River Torrens in a row boat; a miniature tortoiseshell mandolin, bought on the steps of Notre Dame Cathedral in 1924 by Aunty Albertina, and her framed invitation to Their Majesties' afternoon party in the garden of Buckingham Palace (as proof to people who didn't believe it). And I had the china frogs on the mantelpiece, and my painting of Bertie Quigley as "Departing" above them.

I'd been doing something for everybody all my life, and there'd been no time to do much for myself. Those objects needed regular dusting and polishing, and I had six other rooms of objects and a passage full of objects, too, so now I wasn't over at Mrs Packard's I could give them my attention.

I always wore one of my starched pinnies, like I used to at Mrs Packard's. In the cold weather, seeing I was home with nobody to observe me, I'd do my household work in my nice warm imported angora coat, with a waist pinny over it. I had a lot of pinnies: waist ones and ones with a bib that were handy – the only thing was, that if you'd just done your hair and put your head through the pinny hole to get in, you got your hairdo pushed all over the place.

I'd kept Lillie's room just as she'd left it, except I'd straightened out the quilt on the bed. She was fond of dogs and there was a photograph of the poodle she had in Sydney, next to the black and white china Scotty dog money-box with its tongue out; on the chair beside her bed was a toy watchdog like a big white pompom. Lillie was clever with her hands, and I was careful dusting the motor-bike she'd made out of beer bottle tops and the pair of rocking-chairs, twisted out of old baked bean tins, with a bit of her favourite purple colour velvet on their seats.

My sewing-room was opposite the sitting-room and I had Lillie's body model in there and my sewing-machine and my ironing-board and my sleeve-board and my five irons. Hanging from coat-hangers by clothes-pegs were pictures I'd cut out of the newspaper social pages of some of the socialite young ladies I was acquainted with. I had Miss Rosetta Buzzacott attending the Lord Mayor's Ball in strapless raspberry-red Thai silk with a wide hem band of white fur; Mrs Hamish Wavertree cutting her wedding cake with a sword used by her grandfather in the Boer War; Mrs Alasdair Packard, looking a picture, in moonstone-blue pure silk before leaving in the *Himalaya* for her overseas honeymoon; Miss Merridy Angas-Pitcher welcoming the New Year with a loud blast on her toy trumpet . . .

I wasn't hard up, I got my pension, but I did some washing and ironing now and again of different Beauville men's shirts, and matched buttons and changed collars and cuffs. I even did the boss of the Waterworks' shirts; but I'd stopped doing the Count's since he and the Countess moved their School of Social Grace up the hill, and Granpa's house had been knocked down, and the devils turned the space into a used-car yard.

Beauville was changing and Linga-Longa was just about the flashest nicest house in Redruth Street; though Miss Australia had a great big one of those red dogs with only a knob for a tail – a savage big red thing that was always making a dirt on my footpath that was dangerous, because if you trod on it by mistake you'd go for a slide. And once that dog just squatted and had its puppies in the gutter, and an ordinary proper dog would've gone down the bottom of its garden to get a bit of peace and privacy.

But there was so much going on round Beauville – you couldn't even put a cheap broom on your verandah, or it'd be gone in a minute. And Chooky had bought me a marble bird-bath for my front garden, that stood on a stand and had a pipe up through the bottom so it made a spray; and I'd put my biggest china frog in the bird-bath for an ornament, but one morning, so help me goodness, someone came in the night and pinched that blooming frog. I looked round next door in Miss Australia's, and everywhere else I could think of, but I never found it; and the paper-boy watched for me, but we never saw it in anyone's garden, and I never traced that frog at all.

And when you saw the kind of people that went in the

Beauville public ladies' lavatory, if you ever got taken short and needed to go, you'd be very doubtful that you'd want to sit there after them. You'd more likely have to stand up and just go for the best.

The Count and Countess didn't want Joss House when they moved up the hill: they engaged a more elegant houseman to suit their new improved School of Social Grace. So Joss House stayed behind in Beauville, and used his savings to buy a small house in Fifth Street, and supported himself by doing odd jobs round the district.

Joss House did repairs to Linga-Longa, and mowed my lawns and trimmed my fruit trees. I let him pick the vanillafied-tasting old-fashioned foreign fruits with the jelly insides and put them into big cardboard boxes and sell them in at the market, though he liked eating them, too. Joss House gave me some plums off his plum tree in exchange, and I cooked them with sage and they tasted beautiful.

Joss House was always boiling veal bones for his little black puppy, Tulip — he treated that puppy like a baby and was for ever loving her up and petting her, and it gave me the pip. Tulip was all the time scratching herself and making a tiny crackle of blood that got bigger and bled worse; and Tulip would be licking it and making an even bigger bleeding, and turning it into an ulcer. I reckoned Tulip had that disease from overseas, because of people bringing strange dogs into Australia that had lived in the wilderness and eaten wild grass with insects in it that had got into their blood. There were thousands of cases of it round the world and it hadn't been in our country before, till the foreign people came, and it was spreading. And Tulip slept on the end of Joss House's bed at night and I reckoned Joss House had caught the disease and it was giving him his kind of dry throat that made him cough, and sometimes he could hardly talk.

Joss House worried about leaving Tulip in his car while he did his shopping at the market. He asked me to go with him and look after her, so every Friday afternoon I sat in the front seat with Tulip down by my feet. I made her behave and keep still and not be a pest, making smells or scratching or biting or licking; so for once she was as quiet as if she wasn't alive.

Sometimes Joss House was away a long time, because as well as buying his food stuffs he'd get some new socks or underpants or some of his shaving gear, and perhaps have his hair cut. I didn't mind, as I could watch a lot of funny people going by. I'd see fellows with their hair in a plait and beads round their neck and trousers so tight they dug right into their body, and you could see the way of the shape down below. No one ever stared back at me when I sat in Joss House's car waiting for him. Everybody was always very well-behaved when I went out anywhere – men or women or whatever.

I'd give Joss House the money to buy me a jar of good farm honey from the market, and some special yeast bread with raisins in it that was lovely and soft – and it never went green, or if you put it in a tin it wouldn't turn into a hard biscuit while you weren't looking; and it was quite casual – you didn't have to buy a great big loaf, they made it in semi-small ones. And Joss House would buy some lemon cake, though it wasn't a sponge cake; and it was nearly square and a very fine cream colour, and on the top it had white lemon-tasting icing sprinkled with coconut; and when we got back Joss House would give me half for looking after Tulip.

Occasionally Joss House would come round to my place and I'd play the piano, though my fingers had got pretty stiff, and he'd clap, and I'd play some more and he'd sing a song in his strange foreign language. And then he'd tell me about how he'd come through like a leaf which had landed very good – not of his making, but always like a leaf in a river floating; sometimes thrown against the stones and sometimes out further, like a leaf in a stream, thrown against this, and it turned round and so on, and here he was.

Joss House was a real gentleman, as nice to me as he could possibly be. He wouldn't misbehave – no fear; he wouldn't put his hand on you or say anything rude or make any suggestions, or cause you to feel he was looking where he shouldn't. In any case, I wouldn't have wanted to marry Joss House, even if he'd wanted to – what was the good? If a man was polite and you knew him well, and he had a car and wanted to take you somewhere, there was nothing to stop you both from being decent, was there?

They said there was a shower in the sky because the moon was shining too bright. And a lot of the glass windows up near the Hills got broken with the big wind. And bananas got spoilt and made black. And there were some apricots selling in the market today – beautiful ones you could get quite cheap, which usually are dear, because the wind blew the trees that much they rocked them off and made them a bit soft. But if you can squash them and make drinks out of them they're all right. And the late season peaches have been real hard for a while, but the last couple of days they all of a sudden got ripe in the skin. So if you don't split them up the middle and eat them straight away they won't keep.

Though Tulip had the overseas disease, she lived to be thirteen, and after that Joss House didn't get another dog. Joss House's diseasey dry throat hadn't got any worse, but even so many years after he still had his very broad-spoken foreign accent. Because of being bombed about in the War and working hard all his life, he'd started to be a bit overbalanced, and his knees were hurting him from falling over so often when Tulip used to get under his feet. He was always eating little pink pills the doctor had given him to take the aching out of his bones.

Joss House still took me up to the market with him every Friday, and I'd sit and watch the people while he did our shopping. I wondered if some of the fellows I saw were wearing the new tailor-made trouser set I'd seen on the television, with the secret pocket in the fly that had a zipper so they could hide a valuable note there, and you'd have to put your hand inside the fly to find it, and if you did that they'd spit in your eye.

Sometimes Joss House would take me for a drive round the city before we went back to Beauville. One day he showed me Hopedene Street, where I'd lived with Mum and Dad. The Silver Dragon Hotel was there on the corner, but where our house and Dad's garage had been, was a great long showroom, with shiny glass windows, full of the latest model Rolls-Royce type of motor cars.

They'd knocked down a lot of places in Adelaide I'd known for years – if you went anywhere you hadn't been lately you wouldn't know where you were. The streets were cut across and cut through; the map had been sort of run over, so you wouldn't know where to go, you'd get lost in a minute. Rundle Street was gone – they said it was too dangerous for traffic, so you weren't allowed to take any vehicles up there any more; and those funny old priestly looking blokes with the long gowns on who used to go up and down with a drum, banging and playing, were off the street, too. They were knocking down big churches and big shops. Miller Anderson's – that used to have the select costumes in the windows, and was one of the best places to get a nice dress or a hat – was even gone. Adelaide was getting knocked to bits, but what was the good of caring about what you couldn't help.

And down Beauville way it was a wreck. They'd got rid of Uncle Jim's shop, and Sticky Thomas's lolly shop, and Priddle's bakery, and the chemist's shop where the old chemist was so proficient you hadn't really needed a doctor if you had something that was very difficult to understand, as everyone nowadays had some little thing they didn't hardly know how they'd got, or what it was. Everything was going – even lots of nice houses were gone, and I'd never forgive them for knocking down Granpa's.

Joss House always brought me over the piece out of his newspaper with the television programmes on it, and there were some weird things on the telly.

They kept talking about what they were doing, and what they were going to do, and what they ought to do, and a lot of it was what people shouldn't have anything to do with if they were nice people, and the women hardly had any clothes on. Though I supposed in a way it was your mind that made the rudeness up. Because everyone knew what everyone had, without having to undress them and have a look. But they had no privacy whatever on particular programmes, and they told you certain ways of doing things, and, when you thought about it, you didn't realise what a lot of things people had mixed up in their bodies nowadays. People in my younger days weren't sexy like that – if you got into trouble with a man and had a baby you'd be chucked out. Now it was going on constantly. Even the princesses in the royal family were lustified and mucking around. Wanting to get divorces and wanting to be air pilots. The whole place was messy. The little new lady, Princess Fergie, was a very forward person who had a complete driver's licence to take an aeroplane with thirty passengers on board. And Princess Diana and Prince Charlie hadn't got the royal atmosphere; modern family kids like that didn't seem to realise it was a big thing to be the king and queen.

And they were magging about it on the telly all the time: condoms-condoms-condoms. I didn't exactly know what a condom was, but I thought it was some sort of a thing a woman could use on a woman instead of a man, and I'd heard there was a place out North Adelaide where you could buy something like an artificial man's starting-handle. It was going on with people that were highly bred, but you didn't know if someone had something wrong with them, and they mightn't know themselves. You could get some trouble from using a bath or a lavatory. Which was why you wouldn't like to go and use human things belonging to someone else.

A lot of times on the telly, they gave lectures, and the politicians wanted everything their way and were putting the prices up and interfering with people's pensions. Bob Hawke was a cheeky old man, and that woman, Mrs Thatcher or whoever she was, had too much to say – she even argued the point with high men. And the religious people – the churchies – reckoned it wasn't a crime to go with a man if you weren't married, and there was no reason why you had to have a marriage ceremony. There was nothing to it – once, if you were a Roman Catholic and did something wrong, you'd get tossed out; but now the nuns were getting to the priests, and it wasn't looked down upon at all. Once, if you were a nun, you had to be pure but now it was different. Though a nun couldn't have a baby with another nun – they just took them for companions sort of, and it seemed a bit queer. Because they said the Lord gave people sex to go with men and women, not to make fools of themselves and all.

One programme had the women riding bikes, topless – hundreds of them, going pedalling for their life. Another time they showed you how the young people acted health-wise on the naked beaches. The girls didn't have anything on, and they were cuddling and tickling, but it seemed a lot worse to see the men, and you couldn't help looking. Private people who wore bathers were not allowed on those beaches, and if you wanted to go in just to have a look and make a nuisance, they'd pitch you out over the fence.

Now wives had their husbands with them while they were having a baby, and if they thought they were taking too long the husband helped to pull the baby out – I wouldn't have liked Chooky to be there while I was having mine. People were having children or not having them; or having them up-side down or several at a time. And they even showed on the telly how they could take a living embryo and join up the tubes inside. They could change the breed over – from a boy to a girl, or vice versa. I couldn't think about it even. But it was quite possible now, it seemed, to do anything.

Our atmosphere is so intricate because the heat and the cold don't go together, and when they do mix they don't belong to one another. Look at the funny things they put up in the air. And they find things in the ground that have been buried for years, like peculiar rocks and parts of people that they don't know what they are, even. They're finding things they've been looking for for years. And the area of the stars – they've got their own heat, and those people overseas are getting so clever now they think nothing's beyond them, and they're building planes that go so high they get in amongst the stuff up top, and the heat of the stars confuses the planes and they're coming down bang and crash all round us.

When I was young, my hair was a real rich gold colour, like a doll's. Now I didn't have half the hair I used to; and it was a silver colour that was darker at the back than the front.

My hair was still so fine the hairpins slipped out of it, and when I unpinned it, it was down below my shoulders to billyoh. It took a fair bit of drying after I washed it, and I'd sit in the garden and hang my head back over the chair and let my hair blow in the wind. When it was dry I had a job to get it how I wanted it again – I had to comb all the loops and waves out straight, or there was too much to put into my bun. I had a lot of little curls on my neck, but I pinned them under because curls looked silly on you when you were my age: when you got up in a certain age you had to stick to what fitted in more with what you were. But the hairpins wouldn't grip, and when I went rushing out in the garden, the trees touched my hair and pulled it half down. Every time I tried to pick a high-up lemon, the claws in the lemon tree got on me – that tree had little pricks on the edge of its leaves, and if they got caught in your hair you had a job to unwind yourself out again.

Once I was ten-stone-eight, but now I didn't have so much thick meat on me; I was going skinnier all the time. I used to have well-shaped legs and a fairly good bust that wasn't a wobbly thing; and I had brassieres and a corset that did up with hooks all the way down, and on the bottom it had suspenders for the tops of your stockings. But you had to have your figure to fit all that, and mine disappeared – it seemed to just melt. Now I was as flat as a pancake: I didn't wear bras; and I either wore my pantihose or kept my stockings up round my knees with the elastic bands off the rolled-up newspapers.

I didn't eat a terrible lot, though if I ate apricots they chased me round and I kept having to go and see my aunty, but if I ate a lot of chocolatey stuff it made me tight; sometimes I had to have a wee every five minutes, and other times something seemed to tighten up my nerves and not let any blood through, so I felt as if my battery was running down. It was weird, and often I couldn't sleep of a night, but I thought these things happened when people worried you, like that creature next door worried me.

Some people were annoying, they were rotten liars and all the rest of it, and I could have smacked Miss Australia on the head. She told the schoolteacher across the road not to have anything to do with me — she said I was a pest around the place and a stickybeak, and if I came in I'd be pinching things or touching this, that and the other (and he was a nice man, not a saucy man, most polite to me, with a pretty Persian cat, and I knew if I got scared in the night he'd be there in two minutes). But the schoolteacher never took any notice of Miss Australia, he knew what she was, so I said I hoped he wasn't annoyed at my intrusions, and kept on going over and putting his night paper in on his verandah, and his Sunday paper, too; and people left his front gate open that many times a day, and I shut it and shut it.

Miss Australia had got rid of her bluebell creeper, but now she had one of those vines with the red leaves, and when the autumn came the leaves went everywhere over my side fence, and when I complained she said she didn't want it taken away, she liked her privacy, and she put in more and made it that thick you couldn't see through. And one cold day she made me lend her my brand new radiator, and she had it that whole winter, and I had a job to get it back, and when I did it wasn't workings, she'd worn it out. But the worst thing was how she came down in a hurry and said she had to go to a wedding and could she have a lend of Lillie's royal blue beaded dress made by the high people in Sydney for the specialty of what was going on and I didn't say yes or no, and she came in the front door and nearly knocked me over, and rushed into Lillie's room and opened the wardrobe door, and grabbed the damn thing, and rushed out the front door and home with it.

Miss Australia was getting on a bit – she was sixty-odd, but her pants on the line were that tiny, they were only like a little V-piece with a string round it, so if she took a deep breath it'd go up her bottom-hole. She had her dyed yellow hair cut off short and screwed in tight curls, and her makeup painted on, but she didn't look like a woman at all. She looked exactly like a big man dressed up as a woman.

Somebody wrote PUSSYCAT and PASSION FLOWER with their finger in the dust on Miss Australia's car, and she kept driving round with it on. The police said you weren't allowed to have sexy things on the side of your car, because it might distract other drivers and make them run into you.

Miss Australia always had other women's husbands with her, and one night, late, her back verandah light was shining on my kitchen window, so I sneaked a chair outside to the fence and got up on it. I saw Miss Australia sitting there in her nightie with a bottle of beer alongside of her, and there was a man. He was sitting on the other side of the table and I could see he was naked from the waist up, and for all I knew he was probably naked from the waist down, too.

The very next day I found a magazine that was a bit unusual thrown over my fence. I thought the pictures of the ladies' faces on the front were really nice, but when I turned the pages and saw some of those ladies spread out with their whiskers all showing, I thought it was a wonder they were allowed to sell it. It was horrible, it was the dirtiest magazine I'd ever seen in my life, and it said how you could take some sort of pills that made you feel oody-doo. But if those pills made you feel too much that way inclined, you shouldn't take them, because they acted on the nerves, and if people were very much urgent that way, before they knew where they were they'd be kidding with somebody else's husband, or showing themselves to the Milky when he came.

I couldn't put that magazine in my rubbish bin – what about if one of the dustmen got it out and read it? I had to burn it down the back by the tree with golden foreign fruits.

I was the oldest original inhabitant of Redruth Street, because most of the people I'd known practically nearly from a certain time back had gone, and there were new people in their houses. Lots of strangers had come from interstate or overseas – but they were a different breed of overseas people to Joss House.

Next door to me, where the nurse used to be, I had a foreign specialist for funny things you got inside you. Across the road, where Eric Riddle's cousin had been, was an oriental lady who thought she was a doctor with a brass plate on her door, and she treated people whose brains were tired, and if married people couldn't agree with one another she tried to put them together properly. Next to the schoolteacher's were some Italians who had a big restaurant, and one day I could hear something banging in their place, and when I went in it was their electricity-box on the wall with the switches and what-not: the white enamelled door was open and it was banging like mad, and all the switches were on, the little lights were going, and things were buzzing everywhere.

Though they spoke toffy English, you couldn't talk to the new people, because they were complicated sort of people who didn't speak the old Beauville language. And you hardly saw them – they were never home. You might see a light in the night for a while, you might hear a car going out in the morning, but you wouldn't see a soul in the street.

This new lot were forever planting gardens full of gum trees, or putting high walls up, or making swimming pools which were very nice, but you shouldn't have all that moisture among the houses. And there were so many new strange dogs getting round, escaping the animal pick-up man; and dogs weren't allowed loose now, you were meant to take them on a lead, and if they did dirties in the street you were supposed to have a piece of paper to pick the beastly thing up and take it away on, or you got fined (sometimes it was so huge, you'd think a man had done it).

I didn't know why, but, though I still wore a pinny every day, I didn't worry about starching it; and I'd stopped washing and ironing Beauville men's shirts – I'd decided I didn't like anything that took over, and washing and ironing did that and I'd got cross with it. I didn't even feel like dusting Lillie's room or my favourite things. I'd got a mania for being outside in the street, and I was up at a quarter to six every morning and started doing my outside jobs not long after.

Most people in the street didn't know how it happened, but it was me that put everyone's milk in, and picked the newspapers up after the newspaper man threw them and stood them alongside the front doors; and any letters the postman put in people's letter-boxes untidily, so they were all buckled up, I'd straighten out. The biggest job I did was the dustbins: when the dustmen went along, I went along, too; and they were a lazy lot of cows who slammed everything down and spilt half of it, and often a bin would be rolled into the gutter with its lid run away halfway up the road, and I had to put them together and then put them inside their front gate, very gently. I went right up Redruth Street, both sides, doing the dustbins, and when the dustmen looked back they must have wondered where all the bins had disappeared to.

And of course I looked after Joss House a good bit. I went round to Fifth Street to do his dustbin; and I'd put his newspaper on the chair on his verandah; and I got the letters out of his box that was in amongst his hedge, and he usually had a lot with funny foreign stamps, and I put them on his chair, too.

In winter I was going more than ever, because if you didn't fetch people's things in quickly they'd get sopping wet; so I'd be out watching at my gate in between showers, with my pinny on over my coat. I only had little feet and sometimes, hurrying so fast, I swayed and fell and got bumps and all the rest. And Chutney had bought me a pair of waterproof boots lined through with lamb's-wool, and they were lovely and warm, and didn't push on my toe that got squashed by Arnold Bywaters' horse; but they were slippery soled in the wet and could tip you head over heels. One time those slippery rubber soles tipped me up over the little low wall round the schoolteacher's lawn, and my leg was that cold with the weather, it bled like a tap.

One of the new ladies in Redruth Street had her shiny red verandah so polished, I left the marks of my rubber soles on it when I put her milk by her door. After she complained to me, I had to take my shoes off and walk along very close to the wall to get it up on her doorstep without making marks.

And when new telephone books were thrown down I'd put them carefully on people's doorsteps; and if any parcels came for the schoolteacher, I'd take them up to his verandah and leave them by his big pots. Anything that was upside down I put straight: I did all the little odd jobs around for everybody. Most of the people were either asleep or away at work when I did my jobs, and perhaps they thought they were done by a fairy.

This weather is too mad – you can't do what you want to do. Several weeks ago the rain kept pouring so hard nobody could control it really, and gum trees were falling down across the roads because they were old and rotten. The rain was so thick it was making the dirt sloppy, and it was running away with all the fruit and flowers and vegetables. There was so much water that cars were turning over and trains were falling off the lines and animals were being washed into the sea and being eaten by the big sharks that haven't been seen here for years. Those sharks have been coming down into our waters because the people in foreign countries have been frightening them out of their own deep seas.

Sometimes, trying to think back to what you were trying to think, you got a funny feeling in your head. Often, if you put your two fingers on either side, you could feel it tick-tick-tick-ticking – just going like your brain was a clock. The ticking came from two muscles behind your eyes that connected with the nerve that went right through your head and took all the remembering with it. That nerve was one of the main parts of the engine of your body, and if it stopped working you'd have a fit.

It was a blooming business trying to remember it all, hundreds of years back . . . They came from the Bavarian Mountains in the beginning, though some of them might have come off the big islands that were near the pyramids, because the Australians came from everywhere – we were mixed from goodness knows what. And Granpa Rodda came from Redruth in Cornwall, and pushed the

Governor's dog through the porthole; and I was born in 1901, when the Duke and Duchess came . . . and named after two queens . . . and I may, and then again, I may not.

But sometimes I couldn't hardly remember my own name; I almost couldn't remember one day from another; I'd been through so much, so long ago, that I couldn't remember half of what I'd seen. Those times, trying to remember, I felt real queer. I said to Joss House that if he didn't see me around any time, to have a look in and, if I was lying on the floor, I'd probably dropped dead with all this and that I'd had to go through. And I said to tell Chutney he'd better put me face down, or else I'd dig myself out: if he had me buried face down, I'd just dig downwards in the dirt, and wouldn't be able to come out afterwards upwards.

Chutney was the only living close relative in the world I had left; and though I had the presence of Chooky and Lillie, sometimes it seemed I didn't have any family at all.

Chutney was so busy with his boat business and his wife and kids that I never hardly saw him. And when I did see Chutney, he was different from what he used to be when he was young. Sometimes he was that bossified he reminded me of the headmaster who'd dealt with all those rough tigers at the Gilles Street Primary School.

Chutney said I didn't do my laundry-work properly, so he took my towels and sheets away every week for his wife to wash, and then he'd bring them back clean. He didn't like me wearing my pinny over my coat. He wanted to pull out the golden rod that grew tall along in front of the verandah like a curtain. Instead of letting Joss House cut my lawn, he got a strange young man to come every fortnight, who never asked my permission but just brought in his big mower and did it. Chutney seemed to think Linga-Longa was the worst looking house in Redruth Street – he was always complaining about this and that and the other, and saying I'd have to get it done up or get out of it, because it wasn't fit to live in.

Chutney said it was so dark inside the house, that, when you went in, it was pitch like the night-time. And I had proper switch-lights all over the place which you could turn on anywhere; though I didn't like the rooms lit up to billyoh — I liked things semi. So I had the lace curtains at the centre of the windows, and silk ones at the sides; and some windows had blinds with fringes and a tassel on the end of the cord. Though, of course, it was a day when it was raining you had to put on a little bit of light, because it might get too dark inside and if you didn't mind where you were walking you might keep bumping your elbow or something. Chutney got me an electric torch you just switched on or off, and it was handy if I lost an object that ran under the bed or fell down behind somewhere else. But I was scared of switching and pushing lights and things, because if you had too much of that, and it got too hot, you could make a bang and a fire — I was scared of electrics and all that.

Chutney got me an electric blanket for the winter, but I didn't like electric blankets — I'd never gone for hot-water bags or any of that sort of thing; I didn't like extra heat that made you sweat. Even though I often woke up shivery in the night with the cold; and my toes started to itch, and sometimes I had to get out of bed and run up and down the passage a couple of times, because the nerves went and I got the cramp in my hip and my blood thickened up and I couldn't get it going. But I tried to keep myself warm bedtimes in winter by wearing a singlet with sleeves, and a nice soft pair of pants, and my pantihose, and a pair of knitted socks, and one of my jumpers as well as my long woolly nightgown. Really cold nights I'd wear my woollen gloves you could put on either hand without changing over, and they both fitted; and I'd have four travelling rugs on top of my quilt, so it was that heavy I could hardly get under it, and a rug over the bottom sheet I lay on, so when I got in it was cosy; and I made a cape out of a rug with a hole to put my head through, for sitting up in bed. I'd keep turning my pillow over, to stop it feeling cold, and I always pulled it away from the back of my bed that touched the wall, because I reckoned the cold from outside the house came through that wall into the pillow, and even into the mattress with springs. But some nights in bed I'd keep getting sneezes, so I'd have to switch the lamp on beside me, and take a hanky off the dressing-table and blow my nose. What came out was like water, just clear, that didn't hardly make a mark on a pure white handkerchief, only a sort of dent. I couldn't make it out: where was it coming from? Was I leaking from the top of my head? Perhaps I had water on the brain.

When it was my birthday, Chutney took away my black-and-white picture television I'd had for years, and gave me one of those new ones that was supposed to be a very special thing. But I didn't want it, and I didn't like it, and I wouldn't use it. You just sat in your chair and pressed a button, and it came on with pictures all coloured; but there were that many buttons, and you had to push the right one or you got the wrong colour or the wrong picture, and it was very hard to do. I didn't like to have to think which button to push: there were about fifty little different buttons and you had to pick the right one.

So night-times when I wanted to watch the telly, I didn't go in the sitting-room. I went in the kitchen instead, and watched the small set on top of the fridge. But the fluorescent-bar light in the kitchen shone right down on my face, and it was pretty strong, that light. So, to save my eyes from getting tired, I'd sit there with my big sun hat on, that was made out of bamboo thread and was as light as a feather, and you didn't have to pin it on or anything. It made an umbrella almost over me, and I'd sit there on my chair, wrapped up in my raspberry colour fluffy rug if it was cold, because I didn't like electric radiators. I'd have my couple of things I might want for my tea alongside of me, and I'd watch the *News*, and whatever else I might want to see.

My bath was one of those big white ones with lion's paw legs. If you stood up in it when it was wet and slippery, you could fall over and hurt yourself; so when I had a shower bath I'd always put an old towel on the bottom to stand on, and then I wouldn't slip. But I didn't like making a lot of water in the bathroom, slopping round — if you made a slop in the bathroom it was bad. So usually I'd just have a good rub-down scrub bath out of the china bowl with a pattern of nasturtiums.

When I did have a shower bath, the best time I liked to have it was just before I went to bed, and then I was all nice and ready to put my fresh nightie on. But Chutney must have thought I wasn't clean enough, because he got two nurse-girls to come and call on me, and they wanted me to get undressed in the daytime and stand in the bath under the shower, and they wanted to wash my hair and do this, that, and the other, or do something else, and they said they should come twice a week.

It wasn't good to have great boiling hot shower baths all the time — they washed the oil out of your body. I didn't feel like standing up naked in the bath for those two strange girls — oh blow them, no; I was funny like that. Though everybody knew what everybody looked like, if a strip-naked man ever came and stood in front of me, I'd have a fit.

And they wanted me to change every one of my underclothes, and very likely I'd only put the blooming things on fresh that morning. It wasn't as if they were rude or anything, but I couldn't be bothered with them. I'd tell those two nurse-girls I'd had a shower bath the day before, whether I had or not.

But usually they wouldn't believe me, and I'd have the

cramp up my hips from standing still talking so long and I'd just have to have a shower bath to get rid of them.

I didn't eat a lot, I never had.

The Japs ate worms and beetles and all. Even our own Aborigines used to eat those worms as thick as your finger that were full of white fat and weren't poisonous, apparently. Though I supposed if you ate some certain fruit with a worm's egg in it, and you swallowed that egg whole, the worm would crawl out to live inside of you, like an apple seed in an apple.

For breakfast I poured a cup of hot milk with a dash of coffee in it over two and a half Weet-Bix in a soup plate; and I had a piece of the raisin yeast bread from the market with honey on it, and I stirred a teaspoonful of that honey into my cup of coffee. Morning-tea time I'd have a banana, because they reckoned bananas were the best food you could eat, or an orange off my tree; or sometimes I'd cut a grapefruit in halves and put some honey on it, and then cut it a bit with a sharp knife, and then eat it out of the skin, and it was lovely – the taste went right down your throat. And you could get a little parcel of ham, and put some in between bread and butter, and spread on mixed-up mustard or tomato sauce to make a tasty lunch-time sandwich. For tea I might fry two pork sausages brown, and then open a tin of mushroom soup and heat it up to make a gravy; and I had those crackly square biscuits with the dry crumbs that got on the back of your throat and made you cough. And, if you put some hot milk on the milk coffee biscuits with the frill all round them, they swelled up and went like a real pudding.

But Chutney said I wasn't eating properly, and went and ordered me Meals on Wheels. The two old granmas who brought them were sensible ladies, very tidy and polite, but I didn't feel hungry by twelve o'clock when they came; and you didn't seem to still want it in the middle of the afternoon; though it was better to eat early, when you were moving round more, than sticking a great big dinner down your neck, then going to bed (you didn't get the exercise, and then you got constipated or whatever).

They brought me dinners of every description in little silvery dishes. Some of the meat was frizzled all up mostly, but I liked the roast lamb with two roast potatoes, and the mince-meaty sort of thing; and the white fish with no bones and parsley sauce was nice, too, but I didn't have fish very often. And you got a piece of fruit cake, almost like a Christmas cake, or some sponge cakey thing with butter custard; and everything was hot when you got it, but I'd have sooner had the sponge cake when it was cold. And they gave you a cardboard box of orange juice, and you stuck a straw in the corner to suck it out through; and a cup with soup in it, and I always kept the soup for my tea.

But you didn't want to be eating all day long, so I'd only eat some of my Meals on Wheels and give Joss House the rest. He particularly liked grilled stuff, or anything done with onions, and when he went food shopping he'd buy me something in exchange. Or he'd do any small job I wanted done in the garden or the house, and not want any money for doing it. Or he'd invite me to share his specialty foreign dinner dish of some of those big white onions that were delicate when you cut them, like an apple almost, cooked with tender steak and a tomato, or perhaps a slice of pineapple.

We've been having the biggest storms we've had for hundreds of years and a lot of places are being blown away and boats out in the sea are drowning and getting washed ashore. I say it's Armageddon — the whole world's turning over that's been here for millions of years, and it's our original earth that's millions of years old but we don't know anything about it, really. And in the mountains the snow is melting and flooding out places, and the weather's changing gradually up top because of all the water that's getting made down below here. We're interfering with the area up top and that's making the mountains of ice melt and making them run down in water and that's making the sea come in and we're losing all the land of the world round the edges, and I reckon to end up with the sea will go right down underneath everything and the whole world will turn over.

One day when Joss House was up on his roof getting the leaves out of his gutters, he fell off. It was such a bad fall they just picked him up in a rug and rushed him into Adelaide's specialist hospital that was enormous and looked like a cathedral, and everyone that was in a state had their own little square room.

Joss House never came home again. He had to go somewhere to be looked after. I missed him and his queer foreign way, and then his house was put up for sale.

Joss House had been my friend. With him gone I didn't see hardly anyone to talk to, and I was never taken anywhere, and nobody who was a proper friendly visitor came to see me.

Sometimes I felt more than ever as if I had no stuffing in me, or as if I'd got a crack in my nut and was going ratty. Though I kept doing my street jobs and thanking the Lord every night for helping me through the day and hoping nobody was going to go off silly at me, everything I wanted to do seemed to be twice as hard as what it used to be and I often wondered what was the point of it.

I'd always said it was no good worrying about what you couldn't help, but you got such a lot of troubles today that were different to what you'd ever had. And they seemed to knock you flying more – things today were very serious often.

One morning when I went to warm up the milk for my Weet-Bix, the gas wouldn't go on – it just hissed at me, and I got a fright; and I wondered if it was a mistake somewhere and it might explode, and I tried to turn it off and it wouldn't, and I couldn't stop it from hissing; so after a while I plucked up again, and went very carefully back to the hissing and lit a match and it was all right. Another day I couldn't find the key of the back shed that should have been in the kitchen on a hook behind my painting of pink flamingoes hanging on the wall – that key always hung down behind the flamingo picture, but I couldn't find it anywhere, though I looked under the cushions on the chairs and inside of any boxes I had. And strange crawly things ate my purple daisies, and some people said if you breathed in their pollen it went down your lungs and it was bad for you; and my apricot tree went mad and got eaten by worms. Half the time in the winter it was raining in sheets, not spots, and the water was going down the wall and under the floor in my back room, and the floor was starting to buckle up and I was afraid I'd fall through. And Miss Australia was always digging, and squirting hoses, and banging round, and making the ground move so the plaster was rattling and cracking on my walls. And she'd started training my grape-vines to creep up on wires from the top of the fence to her windows, so she could pinch the grapes and keep the sun out of her rooms – and they were my vines, growing in my place. She had her own sort of vines with the red leaves, and those leaves still kept going everywhere, and she'd planted some white flower creeper that leaned on my fence, and the flowers dripped down and made the top of my water tank rusty looking.

All my rushing round and being worried got me going, and I never slept solid. I lay awake thinking about things and wriggling, and as soon as I started to move I had to go on the chamber – I had a nice china one with a lid on it under the bed. When I got back into bed, I'd turn on my portable wireless that you didn't need to plug in, and a bloke would be talking all night, telling you what time it was and what was going on and whether it was going to be fine or what. And I had three clocks in my bedroom, and every clock had a different timed tick.

Sometimes when I went to walk along, I'd roll sideways, bumping myself. One day, putting someone's dustbin in, the gates started to shut on me, and a rose bush caught me and pulled the thread of my pantihose, and then I slipped on my rubber soles and fell over on the path and hit my face and got a cut on my leg that was a nasty one. It didn't bleed a lot, but it hurt and went purple, and Chutney, who was very up in medical things, came and took me to the doctor. I had to pull my pantihose down and sit with my bottom sticking out, and the doctor gave me an injection, and put some very bitey chemicals on my leg and a bandage round and round. And he said I'd cracked my cheekbone, and when they took the X-ray photograph it was like a map with very fine little lines; and my eye swelled up and went waterfied and shut and I couldn't open it.

Miss Australia reckoned to people that I went and looked in everyone's windows – but most of the windows in Redruth Street had curtains, and what the devil would I want to look in windows for? She said I was stickybeaking, and I shouldn't go near anybody. I shouldn't touch people's newspapers; I shouldn't put their milks or their dustbins in for them. "Mind your own bloody business," she said. She said people didn't like me doing it, and yet a few of them had started to thank me.

The worst of it was that Miss Australia telephoned Chutney and told him in not very polite words that I was a nuisance in Beauville. So Chutney came tearing down from his new-built mansion up on the cliffs and said I did too many things when I shouldn't for all the different ones, and he wouldn't allow me to, and so after that I didn't bring in other people's newspapers and milks and dustbins, or touch their letters and telephone books, or anything any more.

I wasn't really unhappy, only I didn't know what to do sometimes. I had tons of objects inside Linga-Longa I couldn't be bothered with, so I started doing a lot of tidying up and chucking out and putting aside, or giving things to someone else.

I gave my Berlin piano and various other valuables to Chutney for him and his wife and kids. I gave my hat with the felt fuchsia buds to the chemist's wife and she looked elegant in it; I gave the schoolteacher's wife one with a white rose on the side that was a dainty thing if you wanted a little touch. I gave away dresses and all sorts of bits and pieces from my sewing-room, but I kept the socialite young ladies' photographs pegged to their coat-hangers even though the newspaper they were printed on had turned yellow.

One day two well-dressed men knocked on my door and asked did I have any things they could borrow to put on shelves in the Art Gallery to display them on view, and people would come and pay to look at them, and the money would keep little children from starving to death.

I let them in the house to make their selection and they admired my artwares and artefacts, and poked through the place, and just picked certain things up and went.

They took Mrs Norbert Packard's goldfish lady, but they grabbed the plastic flowers out of her crystal bowl and dropped them on the floor. They took the oriental incense vase, and the carved hat-stand with mirrors in it, and Chooky's battalion photograph, and some silverware and cut-glass. They tried to take the big Indian brass vase wound round with dragons, but it was so heavy it needed more than two people to lift it up, and one of its snake-god handles snapped off. And they took lots of my other artistic possessions, but none of my paintings, and put them in their van and drove away.

But Chutney said there wasn't any showing in the Art Gallery, and that those men had made it all up. He gave me a right telling off for being so stupid as to let what was part of his family inheritance be pinched. Those two men were cunning and had taken me for a ride.

Chutney took me to the police station, but the police said they weren't able to do anything. Those men had come and just carted my things off. They'd confiscated my valuable artworks and artefacts without proper authority. They'd stolen them, and why the police couldn't catch them and lock them up seemed funny altogether.

They say that soon the world is going to be so hot no one will be able to live in it. They say that our aerial arrangement around all over is going to be that hot that one of these days the whole lot's going to blow up. It's like we're burning in a big rubbish heap, and it's because the beams in the sky and the electrical things in the air have got so big in contents of electricity from the areas above, that they're lighting up into huge diameters of electricity from the sky around, and from the moon and the stars. And that's what's beaming down on the earth. All that electricity in the air is coming in from the areas outside the world itself. The whole land is going back to front again. The whole world is changing over from coldness to heat. Even when you light your gas, instead of burning quietly like it used to, now you just put it on a bit and it flares up and they say a lot of that's coming out of the air – it's coming down from the sky, out of the stars and the moon and the sun. It's a rum go and no mistake.

People all said to me wasn't I afraid to stay in the house on my own. I'd say you only had to die once. The more you worried, the worse it was. I often thought I could hear someone on the verandah at night – though what was the good of getting scared?

Chutney didn't think it right for me to live by myself in a seven-roomed house. He worried worse after those two robbers pinched my things in the daytime. He started saying that if I sold Linga-Longa and went to live in a select place where there were other nice ladies and gentlemen, and I got some friends and company, I'd be a lot happier.

I'd had people asking to buy my house five times – even a doctor had been after it; I could have sold it in a minute. But I'd never seriously thought about selling it. And Chutney might find me a nice place to move to, but I hated the thought of packing up all my things and moving; and I wasn't used to having a whole lot of people around all the time; and there were sure to be some old nurses who'd want to scrub you here, there and everywhere, and put you in a boiling hot bath and then let you out in the freezing cold; and they'd want to massage you and cut your hair and do other things to you, and you didn't want anyone fiddling like that.

But I was eighty-nine years old, I was born when the Duke and Duchess came out, though I felt about eight and nothing half the time. And Linga-Longa's seven rooms were really too big for one person – as fast as I got the house tidied up, something else wanted doing, and what with my sorting out things and giving them away, and trying to manage, I hadn't got a minute to myself. And I didn't like the thought of another winter coming. The passage was that wide and windy it was like Rundle Mall; and then there were all the chimneys on top with the fireplaces down below, and all that draught came down through the rooms. I didn't generally feel that cold in the house, but when you went out in the open the wind was often freezing and blew up your legs so it felt like you had no pants on. And when you came inside you had to screw yourself up or run round to get warm again. But the tips of your fingers stayed cold and you couldn't hold anything: there was no grip in you, and your hands felt they'd gone paralysed or something; they weren't hurting, but they were just not working because of the cold. Your fingers felt like sticks on your hands.

Then Chutney said he'd found some place not far from Redruth Street that was a very special retiring home where I'd be taken care of in every direction possible, and he wanted to take me there to have a look.

One part of me thought I didn't want to go there, and how I wasn't going to have Chutney bossing me and making me sell up all my things inside the house, as well as sell Linga-Longa itself. Another part of me kept thinking how I didn't have any visitors except the nurse-girls and the Meals on Wheels granmas; and sometimes a man knocked at the door and asked if I was a Christian, and I said I hoped so. Nights when I lay awake, not sleeping, the wind in the telegraph wires sounded like babies crying – and I'd think about my little girl baby who died. And the place creaked and groaned, and someone had told me once how they thought it was built on an Aboriginal burying ground, and I wished I had Joss House to talk to . . . But if I went to live in a nursing home they'd want to rub me inside out or upside down or something, and I didn't want people bossing me around – I'd had years of it . . . But what with Miss Australia and her vine leaves and white flower creeper, I'd had too much on my plate. And I didn't know what was up with my nose – stuff still came out in a hanky just like someone had put a bundle of water on my head; I couldn't understand it being liquid like that. And my lips lately had been real dry, as if they had little splinters on them – the dry skin came off just like bits of wood. And I couldn't sleep much – I kept turning over in bed and often I had to get up and straighten my bedclothes, or run up and down the passage for my cramp, or go on the chamber; and sometimes when I got out of bed to peep through the window curtain to see if it was still dark outside, I didn't know hardly where I was because I'd got out of bed the wrong side and was nearly getting up the chimney instead.

The day Chutney showed me the retiring home I wore my knitted costume with the silk lining in it. I could hardly believe my eyes when I saw that it was where Sister Grace Brecknock's Kewpie Maternity Home used to be. It looked just the same out the front, with one of Granpa Rodda's turrets and wrap-around verandahs with iron lacy stuff; but at the back it was rebuilt in a great big round circle like a hotel, with sliding windows and new carpets and lounge suites.

The head lady in charge reminded me something of Mrs

Paris Bertram, and her husband was a Reverend, but he didn't look like one – he was the kind of man you never knew what sort of joke he was going to make on you. He didn't look funny like a real religious man ought to look, he was a bit of a doer: a toffy man in a nice white shirt and a black tie tied in a bow – he didn't come all dressed up like a priest.

The head lady showed me the place where I'd live. It was one of the more exclusive expensive parts like a bed-sitting-room style with its own small kitchen and bathroom; and the bed was a good high one with springs, and there were cupboards and a wardrobe and spaces for any of my bits and pieces I might bring.

Then she took me over to a hall full of old girls doing fancywork or knitting or cross-stitch or making toys or anything; and I could see that with my artistic abilities I could tell them what to do, and it'd be something to look forward to. Because in a place like that you needed a Mistress of Ceremonies to welcome the ladies at the doors; and some had wheelchairs and walking-sticks, and I'd be needed to hold the big strong spring doors open so they wouldn't knock any old lady over; and I'd take them in if there was someone special they wanted to sit with. You got afternoon tea with homemade biscuits, and I could put out the cups and I'd need some new pinnies, because if any butter or cheesey stuff melted it was a job to get it off; and one old girl was aged a hundred-and-two, with pretty white hair, all curly, and she was tidy and you'd never believe it. And up on the stage a lady played the violin, and another one had a beautiful singing voice, but I could play the piano better than the one who was playing – so, all in all, I reckoned I could help that retiring home out quite a lot.

Outside there was a garden with purple daisies just like mine at home; and then the lady in charge took me to where the old gentlemen were, and their hair was well-groomed and some were old soldiers, but there was no silly business – they were most polite to me, and they didn't swear or say nasty things like some of the others I'd known who'd been in the War far over in the East. I supposed some gentlemen might be the old girls' boyfriends, and then next minute one of them jumped up, and it was Joss House. He hugged me round the neck and kissed me on the cheek, and I'd never had that done to me for years.

He said his fall had been such a bad one his mind hadn't been working, and the doctors said he couldn't be left alone in his house any more. So he'd come to the retiring home and he'd wanted to write to tell me, but his sick mind wouldn't let him, and he'd had big needles in him all the time that were agony – they pushed them in and they were sharp, and his joints were out worse than ever, even his ankles; and his spine was twisted, and even now it could go easily out of joint, and over he'd topple.

Joss House said he really liked being in the retiring home. They had concerts where the dancing girls' dresses were frilly with a split up the front, and they did the dances where they whizzed and kicked their legs up above their heads. And you got a birthday card printed in England when it was your day in the Birthday Book, and there were lots of concerts and dinners, and they went down on the beach or up in the Hills in a bus, and had a wonderful time. And they often had people visiting from all over Australia, and some from England and Scotland and different foreign countries. They dressed up like they did overseas, and gave you a lovely afternoon tea, and you didn't have to pay, but you had to be a member of the retiring home to go. And Joss House kissed me again, and said his favourite saying about how he'd come through like a leaf which had landed very good.

There's no moon in the sky tonight.

I'm going into the retiring home tomorrow. Though why they call it a retiring home, I wouldn't know. I'm not retiring – no, not me. I'm starting a new life. But I'm not going to be bossed around. I'll have so much to do – helping with this, that and the other – they may even make me assistant in charge.

Chutney and them have been pulling out a lot of things they think I could take with me. Pulling my private drawers out and having a look, and then I couldn't find that pretty pink box I used to put my two rings in.

I've got all my things ready to take with me – I've got new dresses and nighties and my new pinnies; and I'm taking "A Yard of Cats" and "Departing" and my other painting I did of the Bavarian Mountains with the Tree of Paradise. And Chooky and Lillie will always be with me, even though they won't have the purple lounge suite to sit on.

I'm sorry to be leaving Linga-Longa, but I know it's what's meant to be. Really, I'm glad I'm not staying in Redruth Street because I'm looking forward to starting a new part of my life. And Joss House will be there, and I'll be playing the piano, and I might even start painting again.

Look at the daisies: they were all out today, but now they're shut.

I don't know where the moon is. I think it's gone to bed.

I'm going in to bed now, too.

Good night, Mr Moon.

Other books by

Barbara Hanrahan

Where the Queens All Strayed

"Barbara Hanrahan is arguably the best woman writer to have emerged in Australia in the last decade."

Frances McInherny, *Australian Book Review*

This elegant and disturbing novel follows a young girl's coming-of-age in the Adelaide Hills just after the turn of the century. Thea Hodge, aged twelve, knows that young ladies should be pretty, demure and nice, but what is she to make of the mysterious and sensual Rina, the exotic sisters Love and Mercy, and her own sister Meg, whose plans for marriage and conformity go horribly wrong?

"One of Australia's most stylish, original and sensitive writers."

John Miles, *Adelaide Advertiser*

The Peach Groves

"This is a masterfully chilling tale – horror at its most delightful."
Sally Ramsey, *Times Literary Supplement*

It is 1884 and the child Ida travels with Mama and Maud to New Zealand. The exotic country disappoints the children, until Mr Maufe invites the family to stay with him at his country estate, The Peach Groves. In this, one of her most acclaimed books, Barbara Hanrahan pulls apart the genteel stuffing of colonial respectability, finding instead coarse layers of violence and passion.

"In a word, excellent."

Peter Ward, *Australian*

"Nasty, strange and rather beautiful, *The Peach Groves* is reminiscent of *Picnic at Hanging Rock.*"

Gillian Somerville-Large, *Irish Times*

"There is a variety of characters in this tale, all more or less bizarre . . . hovering on the brink of terror and catastrophe, but all used with a blithe heartlessness to make a most eccentric and exhilarating pattern."

Graham Hough, *London Review of Books*

"*The Peach Groves* pecks shrewdly through the respectable fabric of late Victorian social pretensions and conventions. Coolly savage. Alarming, too."

Stuart Sayers, *Australian Book Review*

The Frangipani Gardens

"Black but luxurious fiction, fluorescent with evil, the work of a gifted storyteller and a lover of words."

Newsday (USA)

In this densely textured and spectacular work of fiction, young Lou Mundy is caught up in the dazzling parties, cafes and theatres of Adelaide high society until she finds another world, of sinister and savage power, behind the radiant facade.

"Hanrahan's most powerful novel."

Alrene Sykes, *Australian Literary Studies*

"Hanrahan is a masterly raconteur, handling her bizarre characters and intricate plots with ease and verve."

Frances McInherny, *Australian Book Review*

"A totally absorbing, transporting novel of sheer literary delight."

John Miles, *Adelaide Advertiser*

"Strange, lyrical Australian novel."

Sunday Times (London)

Dove

"*Dove* is delicately, almost fragrantly written, set in Australia's past, but European in style and content; the life of the individual imagination sensitively declared upon the page."

Fay Weldon, *Weekend Australian*

Dove Sparks had always considered herself someone special. Growing up in the soft safe hills, she was told many times the story of how she had been born amongst ease and luxury in an idyllic valley; how she had been chosen by the rich and fabulous Mrs Arden; and how nasty Valentine robbed her of her rightful inheritance.

Barbara Hanrahan's enchanting novel of a young woman's dreams, personal myths, and twisted destiny marks a turning point in the stylistic development of this gifted author.

"*Dove* is a beautiful work of art with evocative pictures of the natural world . . . a warm, yet strange Australia is on every page, without the sense of sereneness and aridity."

Thelma Forshaw, *Age*

"A vivid, lyrical novel."

Publisher's Weekly (USA)

"Brilliantly memorable . . . the author brings all the themes together in an ending which is dazzling in every sense."

Gwen Harwood, *Sydney Morning Herald*

Flawless Jade

Wing-yee is an ordinary Chinese girl living through extraordinary times. Born during the war with Japan, she experiences the momentous days when Mao Tse-tung's revolutionary changes are sweeping the land. Eventually her family separates, some remaining in Canton while others seek refuge in Hong Kong.

Barbara Hanrahan's new novel is distinguished from her earlier works by its exotic location, and by the broad, impressionistic sweep of recent Chinese history against which she sets, with delicate irony, the sharp and brilliant images of everyday life. The individual voice of Wing-yee, with her brief flowering as Flawless Jade, is invoked in spare poetic language. The personal frustration and national turmoil of the times are countered with humour and hope.

"Wing-yee tells her own story, which engages the reader with its sweetness, honesty and humour, and with the depth of feeling it conveys . . . Barbara Hanrahan's prose has an addictive quality."

Carmel Bird, *Age*

"Her apparently artless narrative achieves strong poetic rhythms, and surfaces that are rich and sensuous, creating a finely imagined China that is also a country of the mind."

Marion Halligan